Praise for William Gay

The Long H

T0151523

"A writer of remarkable talent and
talking about." —*The New York Times Book Review*

"Gay has created a novel of great emotional power." —*Denver Post*

"It'll leave you breathless…" —*Rocky Mountain News*

Provinces of Night

"Earthily idiosyncratic, spookily Gothic…an author with a powerful vision." —*The New York Times*

"An extremely seductive read." —*Washington Post Book World*

"Southern writing at its very finest, soaked through with the words and images of rural Tennessee, packed full of that which really matters, the problems of the human heart." —*Booklist*

"A writer of striking talent." —*Chicago Tribune*

"Almost a personal revival of handwork in fiction—superb—must be listened to and felt." —Barry Hannah, award-winning author of *Geronimo Rex* and *Airships*

"This is a novel from the old school. The characters are truly characters. The prose is Gothic. And the charm is big."
—*The San Diego Union Tribune*

"Writers like Flannery O'Connor or William Faulkner would welcome Gay as their peer for getting characters so entangled in the roots of a family tree." —*Star Tribune* (Minneapolis)

"[A novel] about the preciousness of hope, the fragility of dreams, interwoven with a good-sized dollop of Biblical justice and the belief that a Southern family can be cursed." —*The Miami Herald*

"Plumbs the larger things in life.... The epic and the personal unite seamlessly." —*Milwaukee Journal Sentinel*

"An old-fashioned barrel-aged shot of Tennessee storytelling. Gay's tale of ancient wrongs and men with guns is high-proof stuff." —Elwood Reid, author of *Midnight Sun* and *What Salmon Know*

"A finely wrought, moving story with a plot as old as Homer. Sometimes the old ones are the best ones."
—*The Atlanta Journal Constitution*

"William Gay is the big new name to include in the storied annals of Southern lit." —*Esquire*

"A plot so gripping that the reader wants to fly through the pages to reach the conclusion...but the beauty and richness of Gay's language exerts a contrary pull, making the reader want to linger over every word." —*Rocky Mountain News*

"Gay is a terrific writer." —*The Plain Dealer*

I Hate to See that Evening Sun Go Down

"William Gay is richly gifted: a seemingly effortless storyteller...a writer of prose that's fiercely wrought, pungent in detail yet poetic in the most welcome sense." —*The New York Times Book Review*

"One perfect tale follows another, leaving you in little doubt that Gay is a genuine poet of the ornery, the estranged, the disenfranchised, crafting stories built to last." —*Seattle Times*

"A writer of striking talent." —*Chicago Tribune*

"Gay confirms his place in the Southern fiction pantheon."
—*Publishers Weekly*

"Every story is a masterpiece…in the Southern tradition of Carson McCullers, Flannery O'Connor, and William Faulkner."
—*USA Today*

"As charming as it is wise. Hellfire—in all the right ways."
—*Kirkus Reviews*

"[Gay] brings to these stories the same astounding talent that earned his two novels…a devoted following." —*Booklist*

"Supple and beautifully told tales…saturated with an intense sense of place, their vividness and authenticity are impossible to fake."
—*The San Diego Union Tribune*

"Gay writes about old folks marvelously…. [His] words ring like crystal…" —*Washington Post Book World*

"As always, Gay's description and dialogue are amazing…. Writing like this keeps you reading." —*Orlando Sentinel*

"After two stunning novels that combined the esoteric language of Cormac McCarthy with the subtle humor of Larry Brown, Gay delivers concise craft work in his first short story collection…. Much in the same way Erskine Caldwell created slice-of-life Southern stories that were full of humor, conflict, and even forbidden sensuality many years ago, so now does William Gay." —*The Oregonian*

"[Gay's] strong words never fail to paint a precise picture…. Fans of his novels will find lots of meaty reading here."
—*Chattanooga Times*

"Gay's characters come right up and bite you…. [His] well-chosen words propel the reader straight through his 13 stories." —*Denver Post*

"Even Faulkner would have been proud to call these words his own." —*The Atlanta Journal Constitution*

"Gay captivates with bristling tales of old men, bootleggers, and wife-beaters in rural Tennessee...his prose is as natural and pure as it comes." —*Newsweek*

"This book will have you laughing, fearful, and utterly filled with suspense—often all within the same well-crafted story." —*Southern Living*

"A literary country music song.... With deft and lyrical prose [Gay] captures the poignancy of loss, isolation, and double-fisted grief, of disappointment, rage, jealousy, violence, and heartbreak." —GoMemphis.com

Twilight

"Think *No Country for Old Men* by Cormac McCarthy and *Deliverance* by James Dickey...then double the impact." —Stephen King

"There is much to admire here: breathtaking, evocative writing and a dark, sardonic humor." —*USA Today*

"William Gay brings the daring of Flannery O'Connor and William Gaddis to his lush and violent surrealist yarns." —*The Irish Times*

"This is Southern Gothic of the very darkest hue, dripping with atmosphere, sparkling with loquacity, and with occasional gleams of horrible humor. To be read in the broadest daylight." —*The Times*

Little Sister Death

Also by William Gay

The Long Home

Provinces of Night

I Hate to See that Evening Sun Go Down

Wittgenstein's Lolita/The Iceman

Twilight

Time Done Been Won't Be No More

Little Sister Death

William Gay

DZANC
BOOKS

DZANC
BOOKS

5220 Dexter Ann Arbor Rd.
Ann Arbor, MI 48103
www.dzancbooks.org

"A Fire Burning: An Introduction by Tom Franklin" originally appeared, in slightly different form, in *Oxford American* under the title "William Gay: 1941-2012."

"Queen of the Haunted Dell" originally appeared, in slightly different form, in *Oxford American* under the same title.

Library of Congress Cataloging-in-Publication Data

Names: Gay, William, author.
Title: Little sister death : a novel / William Gay ; introduction by Tom
  Franklin.
Description: Paperback edition. | Ann Arbor, MI : Dzanc Books, 2016.
Identifiers: LCCN 2016012147 | ISBN 9781941088586 (softcover)
Subjects: LCSH: Authors--Fiction. | Fairies--Fiction. |
  Folklore--Tennessee--Fiction. | Legends--Tennessee--Fiction. | BISAC:
  FICTION / Literary. | FICTION / Horror. | FICTION / Fairy Tales, Folk
  Tales, Legends & Mythology. | FICTION / Romance / Gothic. | GSAFD:
  Suspense fiction. | Horror fiction. | Ghost stories.
Classification: LCC PS3557.A985 L58 2016 | DDC 813/.54--dc23
LC record available at https://lccn.loc.gov/2016012147

First paperback edition: September 2016
Interior design by Michelle Dotter

Printed in the United States of America

10 9 8 7 6 5 4 3 2 1

Contents

A Fire Burning:
An Introduction by Tom Franklin

He cut his own hair. In warm weather he'd bathe in the creek behind
his house. He hunted ginseng in the woods when the season was
right. He tended a vegetable garden that grew tomatoes, squash,
okra, carrots, and onions. He smoked Marlboros. He sometimes
wrote in a tree house on his property. Women loved him. They
wanted to take care of him, to fatten him up. In his later years he
never drove. He wrote. He wrote in pencil on yellow legal tablets,
one stacked on another when the first was filled. His favorite
restaurant was Waffle House. In the sixties he heard Janis Joplin
play in Greenwich Village, and when he requested a Bob Dylan
song, she snapped, "We don't do covers, sir." He loved him some
Dylan. He loved *David Letterman*, too, and the Cubs. He loved
Seinfeld, *Deadwood*, William Faulkner, Bill Clinton, AC/DC. His
dogs. He loved movies, though he didn't go to theaters. Most of
all he loved his children, and his grandchildren.

He had high Cherokee cheekbones and small brown eyes that
got lost when he smiled. The skin of his face had deep lines in it
that seemed to hint at hard living. When the writer Janisse Ray met
him, at Rowan Oak in Oxford, Mississippi, she said, "You look like
a man who's been shot at." And he did, he looked like a man who'd
been shot at. There'd be weeks he wouldn't answer his phone. It
might be disconnected, or it might just ring. If this went on too

long, we'd start worrying, his friends, calling each other. Have you talked to William? Have you talked to William?

I met William Gay in July of 1999 at the Sewanee Writers' Conference in Sewanee, Tennessee. My first book, a collection called *Poachers,* had just been published, and I was a fellow at the conference, thrilled to be there with my wife, Beth Ann, who was a scholar. Among the writers loitering about the various events was a man I noticed, often with an attractive younger woman. This man was older but it was hard to tell how much, maybe forty-five, maybe sixty. He looked grizzled. At readings, panels, and parties, he always stood on the fringe, alone or with the woman (his agent, Amy Williams, I'd later learn), and always smoking a Marlboro. If it was noon or later, he'd have a Budweiser.

A few days into the conference, I attended a presentation by Knopf editor Gary Fisketjon. At the end of the talk, I got in line to ask him a question. Waiting, I turned around at one point and there stood the grizzled man himself. He wore blue jeans and a black T-shirt and a navy corduroy sports jacket. We introduced ourselves and I was proud when he told me he'd just gotten my book. He'd seen an ad in the *Oxford American.* He and I began to talk as the line inched along and were still talking when we realized Fisketjon was watching us. William stuck out his hand and said, "I just wanted to meet the man with the balls to edit Cormac McCarthy."

That night, after dinner, I joined William at Rebel's Rest, the house where the afterparties were. We sat in rocking chairs on the porch, me with my Bud Light and him with his Bud Heavy, and he asked my favorite McCarthy novel.

"*Suttree,*" I said.

"Mine too," he said, obviously pleased that I hadn't chosen one of the more popular ones, *Blood Meridian* or *All the Pretty Horses*.

"I love how that book starts," William said of *Suttree*, and then he began to quote the opening paragraph, *Dear friend now in the dusty clockless hours*...and when he stopped I kept going.

Yet it would be months—which was characteristic for William Gay, a man I never once heard brag—before he told me of his own history with Cormac McCarthy.

In the early 1970s, he'd plucked an early McCarthy novel, *Outer Dark*, from a drugstore paperback rack because the guy who'd written it lived in Tennessee, too. William loved the book so much he decided to look up the author in the Knoxville phonebook and was stunned when Cormac McCarthy actually answered. It was awkward at first, and McCarthy wouldn't talk about his own work, but perked up when William mentioned Flannery O'Connor. And then they were off. They spoke intermittently on the phone over the next year, developing enough of a friendship that McCarthy sent William a manuscript copy of *Suttree* before the book was published. It arrived in the mail, coffee-stained, and William read it, then his brother read it, then William read it again and sent it back. This is before one could Xerox, and that copy had been one of the only two. "Or maybe the only one," William said. He also told me that the manuscript contained a scene that was later edited from the novel, a bar fight re-described. McCarthy's marginal note was, "Why re-fight the fight?" William never went to college (out of high school he volunteered for the Navy, figuring the view from Vietnam would be safer from the deck of a ship), so books were his teachers, books and Cormac McCarthy.

After a while, as their phone conversations continued, McCarthy said he gathered that William was a writer. When William confessed he was, McCarthy offered to read his stories. He'd mark the manuscripts and send them back. When I asked William what his edits were like, he said, "I used to like the word 'moon' a lot. I used it four times on one page, and he underlined the first one one time, the second one twice, the third one three times, and by the fourth one he wrote something like, 'Too many goddamn moons.'" From that William learned to intend one's repetition, otherwise it's just clumsy, lazy.

He told me this story late one night in the fall of 1999. I was living in Lewisburg, Pennsylvania, a very lonely Philip Roth Resident in Creative Writing at Bucknell University. I talked to Beth Ann, who was back in Illinois, on the phone each night before she went to bed, and after that I called William, or he'd call me. He'd given me his galley—his only copy of his first galley—of *The Long Home*, and I'd found it amazing, a Tennessee noir (which William pronounced "nar") where the worst sort of character comes to town. As we talked, night after night, he told me about a new novel he was writing, *Provinces of Night*. He sent me the book in manuscript and, as I read it, I realized it was even better than his first.

I was trying to begin my own first novel then, that's why I was at Bucknell in the first place, but I wasn't having any luck. I had a few bad pages. I had a looming deadline. I was growing desperate, and one night told that to William. I said I didn't know if I even had a novel in me.

He didn't say anything for a while, and I opened another beer. Then he told me a story he heard growing up, of a man who tried to steal a ham on Christmas so he could feed his family, and the man he was stealing from shot and killed him. Then the fellow brought the dead man back to his family in a wagon. He pulled him off and laid him on the ground. But he gave them the ham.

I didn't know what to say. The long distance buzzed between us.

"I just thought maybe you could put that in there somewhere," William said.

I don't remember how I responded, but after I hung up, that very night, I wrote six pages, that scene, woman and child waiting and her husband being brought back, shot dead. Along with a ham. As I read over the pages, I realized I had my novel's tone. What I'd just written, I knew, would become the background for one of the characters. And it gave me a foothold. I knew something about her I hadn't before. From there I began, slowly, to write.

Years later, the novel finished at last, William read it for me. He called and said I needed to work on one part. I asked where. He told me the page number. I had one of my poorer sharecroppers in too much misery, William told me. It was the only time I ever offended him, though he never said that. "No matter how hard he got worked," he said, "he'd still want to set on the porch with his kids in the evening. Maybe play a guitar or banjo."

What did I learn? That no character should be a one-note character.

He would say "*Really?*" a lot, his italics, always fascinated or amused by something or other, and it was here his dialect stood out the most. Say the word "Israeli" and take off the "is." That's how he said it.

My wife and I invited him to visit us one of the years we lived in Galesburg, Illinois, and he read "The Paperhanger" at Knox College, where we taught. After he finished, the room packed with students and teachers was quiet. There was a token question, an awkward silence, and so we dismissed. Later, I heard that none of those Midwesterners had been able to understand him, his accent was too thick.

———

Mostly when we talked we talked late at night. He'd be watching *Letterman* or a movie.

"Hey, Thomas," he'd say, the only person who used that version of my name.

If you called him in the middle of the day and let the phone ring and ring, he'd sometimes answer, breathless from having run in from picking tomatoes. But mostly it just rang.

I visited when I could. His son Chris made the best beef stew I've ever eaten. Full of fat carrots and potatoes and onions from the garden. Sitting in their living room, a fire in the woodstove, talking politics or Larry Brown. The Cubs on or, in deference to me, the Braves.

We'd sit on the back porch in summer and look out over Little Swan Creek, which ran behind his house, William scratching the dog's ears, the dog changing as the years passed, first Gus, named for Augustus McCrae in *Lonesome Dove*, and then, after he died, Jude, a sweet pit bull.

In the later years of his life, I'd take my kids to visit William and we'd stand on the bank of the creek, me with a beer, him coffee, and watch as his grandkids joined my children catching small fish on the poles we'd brought, or on their knees in the water after minnows or crawfish or bullfrogs. Jude there, supervising. On those nights Chris would cook for everyone and all the kids, six or seven by now, would fall asleep watching a movie and William and Chris and I would go outside on the porch where Chris would strum his guitar and we'd talk or, later still, watch *Apocalypse Now* again, a film William thought perfectly mimicked in structure the Vietnam War itself, a questionable mission going more and more crazy.

Over the years, we talked. On the phone, on porches, in bars, walking in woods, side by side on literary panels or side by side signing books, in hotel rooms, on a plane, once in South Carolina, where we sat detained for hours because the man with the red Igloo cooler's paperwork didn't match the human organ he was transporting. When the plane finally landed, William, eager for a cigarette, leaned over and whispered, "This'll be the last time you catch me in one of these cocksuckers."

People loved to tell stories about William, and stories about the stories. Mostly they revolved around his being a famous drunk. The funny thing is this: he wasn't a drunk. I've been around a few, and I would tell you if he was. It's interesting that people convince themselves otherwise. As if the myth of desperate, outlandish boozing augmented his talent. Forget those mythologizers: his talent didn't need augmentation. Or as if, by making him such a drunken buffoon, they could then pity him. Forget them all.

They saw him drink at conferences, and he drank at conferences because he was abysmal at small talk. He did not small talk. He did not "network" or schmooze. He was private and it was excruciating for him to stand in a cluster of strangers, even if they were complimenting him. Especially if they were complimenting him. Later, when he began to get famous, he attended a party where, he said, "They perched me on a sofa like a redneck savant. Every time I said anything they all hushed and looked at me. I felt like E. F. Hutton."

He didn't drink much at home. On our early phone calls he would always get a beer, but later it would be coffee. In the last few years of his life, he only drank booze when he went out, when he would get nervous again.

Once (this from writer George Singleton), William was on the schedule at a book festival. He was in the hotel bar, sitting with

George. A woman walks up and introduces herself to William. "You have such fathomless eyes," she tells him. When she leaves, William leans over to George and says, "You'd think, with such fathomless eyes, I'd get laid more."

He had his first heart attack at another book festival, while sitting on a panel.

This from William, and from novelist Bev Marshall, who was there, and Sonny Brewer, William's dear pal, who sat on the panel alongside William:

Someone, a woman, was in the midst of a long, heartfelt question to William, a "question with semicolons" he later told me, when he, William, started to feel shaky. He got cold and began to tremble, began to sweat. Meanwhile, the question was still going on, the woman looking up at the ceiling (I'm imagining now), carefully phrasing each word in the air with her hands while William's heart is racing and he wonders if he's going to pass out or vomit. Or worse.

About then the question ended and the woman sat down and waited for her answer.

William tried to even his breath. He cleared his throat, leaned into the mic, and said, "Sometimes," and the room erupted into laughter.

Sonny, watching William, reported that he lost all color, just went gray. "He looked terrible," Sonny said. "I mean, he always looks terrible, but now he looked even worse."

When he had his second heart attack, the doctors told him he needed a pacemaker.

He said he didn't want it.

"You'll die without it," they said.

"Magnetize that motherfucker," he said.

They did, and it kept him around a while longer. When we'd talk after that, I'd call him an old cyborg and it made him snicker.

Back to Sewanee, 1999.

A bunch of us went skinny-dipping late one night in a pond on a farm somebody knew about. Twenty or so of us clambered into the moonlit water with our drinks, all except my new friend William, whose white shirt glowed on the bank. He paced back and forth, smoking. I'd been talking to Jennifer Haigh for a while when I turned, and there, naked, waist-deep in the moonlight, a Budweiser in one hand and a cigarette in the other, was William.

"I felt a little creepy," he said, "just watching."

Some of these stories have become legend.

How, as a poor kid desperate to write a story, he crushed walnut shells in water to make ink. And wrote the story.

How it got rejected from *The Saturday Evening Post,* a note that said, "We do not accept handwritten manuscripts."

How, once he got famous, the woman he was dating asked to see something he'd written and he gave her "The Paperhanger." He said she would read a while and then look up. Read a while and look up. When she finished it, she asked him, "How much of the paperhanger is you, and how much of you is the paperhanger?" William shrugged and said it was just a story. Made-up characters.

"I don't think she believed me," he said.

The romance ended shortly thereafter.

There's the one about where "The Paperhanger" came from: a plumber who worked a construction job with William when William was younger. The plumber told how he'd been doing a different job, under some rich lady's sink, when her "lapdog" ran in and bit him on the ankle. Before he thought he'd whacked the little dog in the head with his pipe wrench and killed it. Here she comes, clicking through the house in her heels, and he takes the limp dog and lifts out the tray in his toolbox and drops in the dog and replaces the tray, finishes the job. Gets paid. Drives away, flings the dog out the window.

The lesson here, I tell students, is that in "The Paperhanger," William raises the stakes by changing the dog to a little girl. Makes a tragedy out of a comedy.

He loved his long titles, which he said hearkened to Flannery O'Connor. "I Hate to See That Evening Sun Go Down," "Those Deep Elm's Brown Ferry Blues," "Love and Closure on the Life's Highway," "Come Home, Come Home, It's Suppertime," "Charting the Territories of the Red," "Where Will You Go When Your Skin Cannot Contain You?" And even "The Paperhanger," whose original title was, "The Paperhanger, the Doctor's Wife, and the Child Who Went into the Abstract," until, at Sewanee, in 1999, Barry Hannah told him what to call it.

A huge horror fan, William was pleased when one of his literary heroes, Stephen King, chose *Twilight* as the Best Book of 2007 for the magazine *Entertainment Weekly*. King was supposed to call him—William had become friends with King's younger son, Owen, also a writer. The two talked Bob Dylan endlessly, William said. Then Owen told William his father was going to ring him up. For most of us writers, such an occasion would be a career high. Typical for him, William didn't answer. Maybe in his garden.

William had written a short horror novel, he told me. *Little Sister Death*. He'd long been fascinated by the Bell Witch phenomenon in Tennessee, and even had his own encounter with, perhaps, an echo of the Bell Witch herself.

This novel is the most metafictional thing William ever wrote—it's about a writer, obsessed with a haunting, who moves his family to the site. Parts of the book seem to be what Binder, the protagonist, is himself researching and, ultimately, writing. The dispassionate quality of these episodes is chilling. There are paragraphs that shine light into William's own writing process as well: "Binder hated dances but privately he thought he might be able to use it for the book, and if not this one for another. When he was working he always felt hypersensitive to stimuli, to things he ordinarily wouldn't even notice, and later in his manuscripts he would come across things that had brought back moments of remembering, bits of conversation he had overheard, or simply the way someone had looked."

Little Sister Death is also about how a story can seize and absorb a writer and even transport him to dark, dangerous places. How the necessary obsessions of writing can cause its practitioners to risk alienating or losing not only their loved ones but (perhaps) their sanity as well. Many of Binder's traits and much of his history matches William's, who became a very different man from the one his wife married. He would work during the day, as expected, carpentering, painting, hanging drywall, and then go home not to give himself over to his wife. Instead, he'd lock himself in to his true work, writing stories and novels, his wife outside the literal and figurative door, a widow to his craft who left him once their four children were grown, saying she "didn't sign on to be married to John-Boy Walton."

The last time I saw William was in Clarksville, Tennessee, at a writing conference. We stayed up late in his hotel room and talked about the same things we always did. He looked older, frailer. His face was longer and he seemed to have lost weight, though there hadn't been any weight to lose. Yet we laughed and he smoked and I drank my beer and he his coffee and at some point I got up and hugged him goodnight and crossed the street to my sleeping family.

The last time I spoke to him was the day before he died. I'd just put him on speakerphone to a class of beginning fiction writers at Ole Miss, where I teach. For half an hour he told them stories and answered questions. After the class, on the drive home, I called to thank him. I told him he'd been great. They'd loved him.

"*Really?*" he said.

Sonny Brewer told me this next part. William's son Chris told him. That on the night of his death, William made a fire in his wood-burning stove. Then he went across the living room and into his bedroom. He shut the door. And died.

What I wonder is why he shut the door.

Perhaps to keep his beloved dog out. Perhaps because he was so private. What he had to do he had to do alone. He went in and closed the door and I imagine Jude outside it, whining, scratching at the wood. He worries something is wrong. And something is wrong. It will keep being wrong.

But I also think of this when I think of William Gay. He built us a fire, he left it burning.

Little Sister Death

And Hunger and Pain drew subtly nearer, and there in the water was one all young and white, and with long shining hair like a column of fair sunny water…. And the tree covered with leaves of a thousand different colors spoke and all the leaves whirled up into the air and spun about it; and the tree was an old man with a shining white beard like a silver cuirass, and the leaves were birds.

What sayest thou, good Saint Francis?

"Little sister Death," said the good Saint Francis.

—William Faulkner, *Mayday*

A Plantation in the Tennessee Country, c. 1785

The wagon and team came jouncing and creaking around the foot of the hill and up the dry creek bed, but the portly man in the black broad-brimmed hat and the dark suit didn't know that. He sat huddled in the corner of the wagonbed, blindfolded, arms clutching the sideboards in a vain effort to absorb the shock of the hard bouncing over the rocks, the wagon tilting up and then ascending the bank and him sliding against the tailgate and the black Mastiff growling at him deep in its throat and shifting position slightly on the jarring wagonbed, its chin laid between its paws, watching him.

He had stopped wondering where he was. He knew from the crying of the whippoorwills that night had fallen. He knew that the ground was frozen, for he could hear the iron rims of the wagon wheels turning against earth frozen in icy whorls. He knew that he'd been in the woods; a branch had rapped him hard and cut his face, a trickle of blood had frozen, crusted like a scarlet slash from a solitary fingernail.

The heavyset man, whose misfortune it was to be a doctor of medicine, was blindfolded with a winding of muslin that covered his face from the tip of his nose to the felt of his broad-brimmed hat; the hat itself jammed on his head misshapen, the brim uncurled and splayed out as if someone had laid a hand to each side of the hat and jerked down hard. Which was, in fact, what had actually happened. The white man with the muttonchop whiskers had leant toward him for a moment, stooping to attain eye level, then performing what the doctor saw as the final insult to his dignity (he had not known there was more still to come): grasping the hat and yanking it down until it seemed stopped only by the obstruction his ears formed, the whiskered man's face showing all this time only a sardonic amusement.

They were three in the wagon, not counting the Mastiff: the portly doctor, a rawboned man with muttonchop whiskers and a flatbrimmed countryman's hat, and a gangling black who seemed to be dozing on the seat, slack lines paying out from his hands to the team of horses left to their own discretion, or perhaps following some nigh-invisible trail to a place they knew.

The doctor, whose name was Mayfield, had stepped out of his office in Mossburg, Tennessee, at ten o'clock the morning before, and the black, who had been folded against the wall by the door, had arisen with an inherent gracelessness, like a carpenter's rule unfolding itself. The Negro had on a dusty shapeless cap he did not doff, and when his eyes met the doctor's, there was no deference in them. He said, Old Marster say he need to talk to you.

Turning, the doctor saw for the first time the man in the flatbrimmed hat, his upper lip was shaven clean but he wore a neatly trimmed white beard and muttonchop sideburns on his florid face, and his silver hair curled out from beneath the brushed hat and obscured the collar of the broadcloth coat. The look of a gentleman or at least a country squire. The doctor nodded to him and started a smile but something in the man's face precluded it. He saw immediately why a doctor was needed. There was something wrong with the man's mouth. It seemed swollen from the inside, so grotesquely that the face seemed deformed. The purple tip of a swollen tongue protruded between his lips and the cheeks looked peculiarly distended like nothing so much, Mayfield thought, as if you had sharpened the ends of a stick four or five inches and jammed it into the man's mouth and forced him to clamp it between his teeth.

The man said something preemptory to him but Mayfield had not an inkling of what he had been told to do. Then the black took his elbow roughly and turned him toward a wagon hitched and waiting at the curb.

Old Marster say you come on, he said.

Mayfield knocked his hand away. Keep your hands to yourself, he said, but the Negro showed no offense. The black, shiny face was impassive save the yellow-looking eyes where glinted a detached light of amusement.

He was being forced toward the wagon.

Sick folks, the black man said. Sick folks need lookin after.

Sick folks? Where? What the hell you after, anyway? Is it his face you want seen to?

He was at the wagon, could smell the horses, a Mastiff across the straw-strewn bed, sleepyeyed yet watchful.

Where are these sick folks?

The white man nodded. Bout a day's ride, the black man said.

That's out of the question. Get your own doctor. I have patients in Mossburg to attend to.

No one said anything.

Is it an emergency or what?

The white man said something indecipherable and Mayfield looked at the black man's face. The black was grinning, his crescent of yellow teeth like grains of corn. Mare foaling, he said.

Mare? By God! I'm not a goddamned veterinarian, I'm a—

The big white man had advanced and abruptly he shoved him, slamming Mayfield against the wagon, knocking his hat into the street. The horses stirred and subsided. He looked up. The man was standing over him, the broadcloth coat open. There was a pistol shoved into the waistband and his hand loosely clasped the grip.

Mayfield got up. He looked up and down the street. It was ten o'clock on a Sunday morning and there was no soul about. He stooped and picked up the hat, brushed it off with his handkerchief. That was when the man had taken the hat and jammed it on his head.

As they went past the city limits and into open country, the doctor said, Folks'll be looking for me, you know.

The whiskered man said something. The black turned toward him. Old Marster he say you hush your mouth, she ain't missin you nothin to what she goin to.

He sat silent in the wagon and thought about his wife. She was waiting to go to church. He thought of her opening the door, looking impatiently up and down the road for him. The day wearing on, her worry mounting. After a while he tried not to think of her at all.

At noon they stopped where there was a stream. The horses drank. They were in a sylvan wilderness, a place that seemed never to have known human habitation. The men had something in a bag: food, biscuits, some kind of meat. They didn't offer him any. The Negro ate in a silent concentration, his jaws working over the tough meat. The white man tried to eat and couldn't and a rage seized him. He swore and threw the bread and meat at Mayfield, the biscuit striking him in the face.

They went on, and when they passed what Mayfield knew was the last cabin they blindfolded him.

He was asleep when the wagon stopped. He awoke sore and cold and disoriented at the abrupt cessation of motion and the ending of noises. He couldn't number the many hours of the monotonous creaking of the springs, the grinding of the wheels on the frozen ground.

Rough hands at the binding of muslin and the blindfold fell away. The moonshine was black and silver, blurred from hours of darkness like an ink sketch left in the rain. His vision began to clear. The dark earth glittered with hoarfrost.

Light, the black man commented.

Mayfield climbed over the tailgate and fell against the wagon, his legs asleep. He righted himself and turned to look about.

He still had no idea where he was but he perceived dimly they'd reached an area of human habitation. He could hear the lowing of cattle, a dog somewhere barking. He had a vague olfactory sense of woodsmoke, a barn, an outhouse.

The cabin they led him to had no furnishing save a bed. He could see that much by the moonlight, then the door closed behind him and he was shut into a windowless darkness, a spiderlike negation of light against the paler black. The air in the cabin was fetid with the sour stench of sweat, old unwashed clothing, the stale smell of burnt-out fires, the odor of rancid grease.

He shoved angrily at the door but it had been latched in some manner from the outside. He lay wearily on the bed.

After a while the door opened and a heavy Negro woman came in carrying in one hand a kerosene lamp and in the other a plate. She moved slowly, deliberately, her face vacuous and benumbed as if she had been roused from sleep. She reached him the plate and he took it and sat on the side of the bed holding it. He could smell fried sidemeat, field peas. The angular black man stood in the doorway watching him.

Where am I? Mayfield asked the woman.

The woman didn't look at him. Why, you right here, she said. Where did you reckon you was?

He awoke sometime in the night scratching all over from the bites. He could feel something verminous crawling about under his clothing. He got up slapping at himself. You filthy little son of bitches, he said, half sobbing, uncertain even as to whom he was talking. He took off his coat and rolled it into a pillow. He lay down on the floor.

In the morning there was more food, grits and greasy eggs fried hard and rubbery, their edges seared to frail black lace. He spoke to the woman but he might have been talking to the wall for the response he got. Later the man with the muttonchop whiskers and his black interpreter came. The man wanted something done for his mouth.

Mayfield had his bag, but there was nothing in it for such as this. Worse yet, there was nothing in Mayfield's knowledge or experience for it. He didn't know what it was. He didn't even suspect what it was, so he did what doctors have done since time immemorial when they don't know what else to do: he put on a confident manner and he swabbed the man's mouth with antiseptic and hoped for the best.

All right, he said to himself when they had gone, I am stuck here at his beck and call. I am the house doctor, and they will keep me here feeding me grits and eggs you could half sole shoes with. Either that or whatever it is gets well on its own or eats the son of a bitch's whole head the rest of the way off, either of which ought to result in them turning me loose.

He could find sense in this, of a sort. There was logic here, the reasoning of a functioning mind. Anything was better than yesterday. Yesterday had been random, senseless, as uncontrollable as the spill of dice from a cup. He had known in his heart they had been riding him to his death, though why they had blindfolded him was just another piece he could not explain.

He doctored the man's mouth three more days, keeping track of the passage of time by the trips the woman made bringing meals and by the difference in the sounds he heard, then on the fourth they came for him in the middle of the night.

It was cold and spitting snow, he could see its slow slant by the lantern light. They passed between the cribs of slavequarters, the trunks of enormous live oaks pale and transparent-looking in the rolling fog. They went toward a house built on an elevation and silhouetted black against the slightly paler sky so it looked depthless, a false front with rectangular knockouts through which dim yellow light flared.

A story-and-a-half log house with a dogtrot between two sections of rooms. He was led up a dark stairwell to an attic bedroom, ushered through the door. It was warm and comfortable in the room, the first time Mayfield had been warm in four days. An enormous fire crackled in the fireplace and fire logs were ricked in against a stone woodbox.

There was a brass bed in one corner of the room, on which a young girl lay partially covered with a blue sheet. Her long hair was the color of cornsilk. She seemed to be very young. She was watching Mayfield with wide blue eyes, a look congested with a mixture of fear and horror. Through the sheet he could see that she was grotesquely pregnant, and he divined at last the true reason for his presence, though not the methods that had ensured it. He set the bag down at the foot of the bed.

You men get out of here, he said, feeling better and more confident, at last in a situation he felt master of. A set of cir-cumstances experience and training had made him familiar with.

The black man turned and went out and closed the door behind him. The white man said something. The malady that had affected him seemed to be dissipating. His face was not nearly as swollen, and Mayfield was able to understand a few words he told the black woman. Nonetheless the woman turned to him.

Old Marster say he ain't trustin this gal to no nigger midwife. Says it's a life for a life. He say tell you if she dies you die too.

The whiskered man said something else.

The heavyset black woman sat by the bedside, her face a gargoyle of sorrow, statuary carved with infinite care from black ebony. Mayfield turned the sheet back, and she fought him weakly so that he thought to himself, well, little lady, if you'd fought over the cover that hard nine months ago, me and you wouldn't be doing it now. He uncurled the girl's fingers from it, her eyes blank and then altering to a kind of bitter spitefulness. As if it was all his doing, as if she blamed him for planting the seed that he had been kidnapped and bounced blindfolded in a wagon a hard day's ride to harvest. He watched her eyes, then abruptly a whine of pain assaulted her so that she clenched them tight, made a soft mewing sound like a cat. He shoved the gown up till it swaddled about her hips. Her water had broken and the bedclothes were stained a pale rose pink.

The man sat on the hearth, and with a hawkbilled knife he cut himself a childsized sliver of chewing tobacco and inserted it in his rosebud mouth, worried it about irritably as if it brought him small satisfaction.

When the birth happened, it happened without incident, almost anticlimactic, and Mayfield felt a curious sense of disappointment, as if he had been brought this far for nothing. It was a boy, beetred and squalling and wrinkled, a full head of sandy red hair.

Mayfield washed him with soap and water the old woman brought him, wrapped him in a clean muslin shift. The girl slept.

The old woman sat holding the baby until the rawboned man got up from the hearth and strode toward her. She watched him with a growing apprehension.

He held his arms out for the baby, but something did not look right to Mayfield. He knew intuitively the scene was darkly parodic, not what it seemed. The man said something short and guttural, a curse or an invocation. She reached the child up to—what? Mayfield wondered. Grandfather? Father? Then he dropped the pan of water he was holding and screamed, for the man had turned and thrown the baby into the fire.

Mayfield's scream was the inchoate, anguished scream of an animal, outraged, an appalled venting of sound bordering on madness. He crossed the room in two strides but the bearded man blocked his path. He seized the man by his face, his features going utterly vacuous with pain when Mayfield hit his cheeks, the eyes rolling upward and his breath wheezing with an audible hiss.

Mayfield had his thumbs locked in the soft depression of the man's throat when the door opened behind them. The black man leapt upon Mayfield, fairly swinging on the thick arms to disengage them. The man with the muttonchop whiskers stumbled backward wildeyed, arms flailing, ceased when he remembered the knife.

He stepped forward, instinctively positioned his feet just as the gangling black's arms encircled Mayfield's chest. The hawkbilled knife flashed in an arc above them, hooked the point of Mayfield's jaw, and ripped open his throat, forming there momentarily a grotesque second mouth that vanished abruptly in a gout of blood that spewed down his white shirtfront and over the black man's arms, and when the black released him he dropped slack and resistless to the floor.

Tennessee, 1956-1965

The logistics of chance had always fascinated David Binder, the curious inevitability of coincidence prevailing over the odds. Jung called it synchronicity, and after Binder read Jung's book he was wont to call it synchronicity too. He was fascinated as well by the little incidents in life that appear wearing masks, disguised as other incidents; years later their significance surfaces, and sometimes you remember, with a sense of déjà vu, the keystone event that triggered the sequence. More often you don't.

If you had asked David Binder to name the events that led him to the Beale farm in southwestern Tennessee in the summer of 1982 he might have named any but these:

In 1956, when Binder was six years old, he came in from school and went into his living room and there was a strange woman in his father's rocking chair. The woman was old, seventy-something perhaps, and it was obvious even to a six-year-old that something was amiss. Her clothing was oldfashioned, years out of date. She was a heavyset woman in a black bonnet that tied beneath her chin, a long dress of some thick dark fabric he wasn't familiar with, and he noted dispassionately that her hightopped shoes buttoned instead of tied. All in all she looked like some old yellowed daguerreotype from the bottom of the picture box.

It was a moment curiously electric, and he was simultaneously aware of a myriad of conflicting images. The woman's face, unaware of him, was highly colored, almost florid, and she had rheumy blue eyes. A wisp of irongray hair peeked from beneath the bonnet. He turned. Through the open window he could see his mother in the garden, the rhythmic swing of the hoe, hear its metallic chink against the earth. The old woman motionless in the motionless chair, and the hot July day itself suddenly frozen, as if time had paused a moment to catch its breath.

When he turned from the window she was gone.

Binder was already known as an imaginative child. Nobody believed for a moment that he had seen a woman in the living room. Nothing happened to call it to mind later: no telegram, no phone call in the night, no longdistant relative unexpectedly dead. It was random, insignificant, purposeless. In a few hours' time his parents had forgotten it; within the week he had forgotten it himself.

It was nine years before the next incident. He'd had a bitter argument with his father, both of them shouting themselves into a rage for neither the first time nor the last. All the same there was something different about it. A shower of stones fell on the roof. He could hear them striking the shingles, rattling hollowly in the gutters, and he ran outside. Staring in disbelief, he could see them forming above the roof of the house, round white stones half the size of an egg. Binder picked one out of the grass and cupped his hand about it. It was warm to the touch.

A week later he left for baseball camp. That had, incidentally, been what the shouting match was about. The shower of stones was forgotten. He never thought of it again.

Chicago, 1980

They were living in an apartment on Clark Street in Chicago when Binder first began to feel he was living out the balance of someone else's life. They had married his second year at the University of Tennessee and he immediately dropped out. He had to have more money. Two, it seemed, could not live nearly as cheaply as one, especially if that one had been accustomed to subsisting on whatever fell to hand, spending what little money he did have in secondhand bookstores. There seemed to be precious little money in Blount County that year, and none he could lay hands on.

He went to work in Corrie's father's furniture store, but that hadn't lasted long. Then he went to work for a garment factory. That lasted a little longer. All this time he was writing. He began a novel, abandoned it. Began another, wearied of it. After eighteen months the factory shut its doors and Binder was out of a job.

For decades Chicago had been the gateway to another sort of life for the rootless of the South, and so it was for David Binder: he found a job first week there and in one month sent for Corrie.

Binder worked days as an assembler in a plant that made gauges for aircraft. He had enrolled in night classes with some vague idea that he might become an English teacher, Corrie enrolling just to be with him. They had little time for each other, for Binder was writing another novel in his spare moments, writing it without knowing why or even believing that it would be read by eyes other than his own. While he played at writing, Corrie played at housekeeping, pregnant already and little more than a child herself, unsure and willing to settle for whatever time Binder could give her. Binder was living on the edge already and knowing it, knowing that he was spending time like money he might not be able to replace.

In two years' time he would have achieved enough distance to look back on it with nostalgia, to remember it as the best of times, days and nights filled with purpose and ambition, but he did not know that then. Not in the dislocated otherworldly hour of two or three o'clock in the morning when he would put away the typescript and look at the clock with a grim foreboding, a man on a losing streak sweating the last card in a hand of five-card draw. Nor would he know it the next day, listening to the jungle of machinery, hypnotized and robotlike, his hands doing the selfsame job over and over until they seemed divorced from him, appendages that could have functioned as well without him.

When he finally stood looking down at the neat stack of typescript he had not an inkling of what to do with it, but having invested so many hours typing it and untold hours writing it and thinking about it, he knew he had to do something.

For no other reason than that he was a devotee of Faulkner, he sent it to Random House first. He and Corrie made a small ceremony of the trek down to the post office to mail it. One of the stamps the postman affixed to it bore the likeness of Eugene O'Neill and Binder wryly took that as a good omen.

In reality he expected to wait two or three months and get the manuscript back with a polite note of refusal; he was already trying to decide where to send it next. That was not the way it happened.

Scarcely a month later Corrie handed him a letter from Random House. Her face was white and solemn. She had opened it. He stood in the doorway, still holding his lunchbox, looking down at the letter, and he was suddenly afraid. He was afraid they weren't going to buy it. He was afraid they were, and he realized intuitively that his life was going to alter drastically and he didn't know whether he wanted it to or not.

Oh, Jesus, he said.

Open it, she said. Oh, David, I told you so. I told you you were good.

The letter was from an editor who had liked the book and was full of cautious enthusiasm for it, though they did not feel that the book was the sort that would be a great commercial success they were certainly impressed with his ability and they felt he had the potential to become an important writer.

In effect they were willing to gamble a five-thousand-dollar advance on the book. If Binder was amenable, a contract would be drawn up.

Binder was more than amenable, and the next two years seemed a curious dreamlike altering of time, as if his life was a clock running a shade too fast. The book was published to a virtual world of praise. It was almost unprecedented for a first novel to be so well received. The only note of reservation came from a reviewer for the *New Yorker*, who, though giving the book grudging praise, thought Binder dealt with the morbid and the dark shadings of life perhaps a bit too lovingly. Binder barely noticed this sentence at the time, but two years later it would creep up from his subconscious and come back to haunt him like a curse or a Gypsy seer's halfforgotten prophecy fulfilling itself.

The book didn't sell well. In fact it barely earned back the advance, but it went on to win the Faulkner Award for the best first novel of the year, and coincidentally the not inconsiderable monetary sum of ten thousand dollars.

Binder was ten feet high, and he guessed for a Tennessee boy he was chopping in mighty tall cotton. He and Corrie had a better address now and were even thinking about moving back to Tennessee. They had more time. Binder had dropped out of night school. He had decided he didn't want to be a schoolteacher after all, and on days when he felt he needed a little something to cheer himself up he had only to drive out to the Stewart-Warner plant in the industrial park and listen to the sound of metal perpetually flaying metal and watch the folks file in and out with their lunchboxes in their hands, and know he didn't have to.

He was working on his second novel, and when he finished it he boxed it up and consigned it to the US Mail. He thought it had gone pretty well and he took a few days off for a welldeserved rest and waited for the check to come rolling in.

There was silence for a time, as if he had walked onto a pier and dropped a box into Lake Erie or dispatched it to the voids of windy space. Then finally he heard. Up there in New York they did not think the book went quite as well as he had: in short, there were faults. Structural faults, stylistic faults, the ending didn't work. And perhaps another title?

He sat rereading the manuscript with the cold clarity of distance and he was reading it with eyes that seemed to have the scales only recently fallen from them. What a ghastly piece of shit, he thought, possessed with a sardonic sense of amusement, as if someone else had written it. Poor, deformed thing from its mother's womb untimely ripped. Looking at it now he realized he had written it out of the sheer necessity of stringing words together. Having written one novel he felt compelled to write another, whether he had anything to write about or not. Hadn't the reviews called him a novelist? He began revising it, but it seemed cold and lifeless, as dead as a letter turning up with a postmark ten years gone. He sat staring at the typewriter but his mind wouldn't work. Someone had unplugged it, had left the switch on, and the battery had run down, he thought.

The beginning of summer in Chicago that year was fiercely hot. You could feel the sidewalks leaking back the sun through the soles of your shoes. The Windy City lay breezeless and heatbenumbed. Binder took to sitting in a bar on Clark Street and watching the Cubs play baseball on TV and drinking ice-cold beer. The Cubs weren't having that great a year either.

Along the way he had acquired an agent. Her name was Pauline Siebel and she was a large, plainspoken woman whose motherly manner belied the stubbornness beneath it, like spring steel deceptively upholstered.

Through the glass door of the telephone booth he watched the patrons of the bar going about the serious business of the day's drinking, Pauline's voice a reassuring buzz in his ear, businesslike. Somewhere out there in the world folks were still doing things.

Look, she told him. If you can't write the damned thing then you can't write the damned thing. Put it aside, work on something else. Begin another novel.

Binder smiled into the phone but the smile felt strange on his face. Right now I don't know another novel, he said.

All right. Then don't write one. Did you save any of the money?

Very damned little.

Then you'll either have to go back to work or write something saleable. You're a writer, aren't you? You said you were. A compulsive writer? If a compulsive carpenter couldn't build a

Moorish castle he could still build a chicken coop. Even with a chicken coop there are variations in quality.

What do you mean?

Write a genre novel. Write *Shootout at Wild Horse Gulch* or *Trixie Finds Love in the Bahamas*. Write something we can sell to the paperback house. Write a horror novel. The two books I've seen of yours have that mood, those overtones to them anyway. The softcover racks are full of horror novels.

I don't know if I could do that or not.

Are you saving yourself for posterity or what?

I guess I don't know if I can do it.

Well, Pauline said, a shrug in her voice, you're a writer. It's your decision to make.

I'll write you in a day or two and let you know.

By the time he got back to his beer and the ballgame, his mind was already busy thinking of a ghost story. He couldn't focus on the ballgame. He always enjoyed reading M. R. James and H. P. Lovecraft and Shirley Jackson's *The Haunting of Hill House* was one of his favorite novels. Binder, in his youth, had always been interested in the supernatural, had felt some deep and nameless affinity for the questions that did not have any answers.

Halfdazed from the heat and from the beer he'd drunk Binder went into a used bookstore on Clark and began to browse. He bought a halfdozen books from a shelf marked OCCULT ARTS AND SCIENCES, selecting volumes with no criteria save their titles, choosing those with ghost or haunting or poltergeist, passing over those on astrology and spiritualism and out-of-body contact. With the paper bag of books under his arm he turned into the first bar he saw and ordered a Hamm's, took it and the books to a back booth under the air conditioner, and studied them critically.

Not much here. *Ghosts in American Houses. Fifty Great Ghost Stories.* He hesitated on an oversized paperback, for the title stirred some memory he had lost. The book was covered with thick red paper, typescript in black, no illustration. It had been published by some house he had never heard of, one he guessed was out of business long ago, or perhaps the book had even been privately printed by a vanity press.

The Beale Haunting by J. R. Lipscomb. J. R. Lipscomb was not given to modesty, Binder figured, for the book was subtitled: *The Authentic History of Tennessee's Mysterious Talking Goblin, the Greatest Wonder of the Nineteenth Century.*

He opened the book and with a shock of recognition saw an ink drawing of a girl, buxom and distraught, the words beneath: VIRGINIA BEALE, FAERY QUEEN OF THE HAUNTED DELL.

He suddenly remembered the Beale haunting, saw immediately that fate, coincidence, and synchronicity had played into his hands. This had happened in Tennessee, two hundred miles and a hundred years from his home. He remembered an old issue of *Life* magazine from his childhood, a Halloween number with an article called "The Seven Greatest American Ghost Stories" or something of that nature. There had been two pages on the Beale haunting.

That night he read the book cover to cover, then lay sleepless thinking about it, his brain striving to postulate a solution. It grew in his mind, tolled there some evocation of familiarity until he found himself obscurely homesick for a place he had never been.

The book was amateurish and extravagantly overwritten and mawkishly sentimental in its treatment of the Beale family and their travails, but Binder was fascinated. It was a clear case of material transcending style. On the surface it was a story of a family's relocation from North Carolina to Tennessee in the first half of the nineteenth century. It was a piece of history of the Tennessee wilderness, a story of pretty, teenaged Virginia Beale, whose wellordered life was shortly to be shattered. The tale deepened and darkened with the advent of the haunting and the ultimate descent into madness and bloody violence. Beneath the surface it seemed to Binder saturated with erotic Freudian symbolism, and he wondered if anyone had ever read the book in quite that way before.

He had to write a book about it; it seemed an unmined wealth of material. He wanted to let his mind play with the facts, rearrange them to his whims, find answers to the questions of rationality the book raised. A plan had already begun forming in his mind. He was burnt out on Chicago, had no desire to be here when the hot brassy summer changed to wind and snow.

The next day he bought an atlas of road maps. There it was. Beale Station, Tennessee, population 2,842. He could hardly believe it. The story had read like a dark fairy tale. It was like looking on a map and finding Magonia, leafing through a telephone book and finding a listing for Borley Rectory.

Beale Station, 1982

The real estate agent was named Greaves. He was a heavyset man in hornrimmed glasses and he had the professional gladhanding air of the successful businessman about him. He sat behind a desk littered with deeds and plats and advertising brochures, chainsmoking Lucky Strikes and drinking tepid coffee out of Styrofoam cups.

Yes, sir, he said. If banker Qualls told you that then he told you right. I have the only section of the Beale farm that's available at any price.

The banker said the place had been split up quite a bit.

Oh my, yes. Originally it was over sixteen hundred acres, but that was way back in the eighteen hundreds. The only remaining section that could be called the Beale farm runs only sixty-two acres, but the house has been continually maintained and I guess you could call it the old homeplace.

The house? You mean old Jacob Beale's house? I understood that was torn down years ago.

No, no. Well, the original log house was torn down, but Beale had another house built, a better one. He lived there until his death and then his son lived there. Of course the house has been renovated, wired and plumbed and that sort of thing. Are you interested enough to drive out and take a look at it?

That's why I'm here.

Greaves arose. And that's why I'm here, he said.

Outside it was blinding hot, the sun searing white off the decks of parked cars. The sky was a bright cloudless blue. Binder paused to put on sunglasses, Greaves clipping dark lenses over his spectacles.

We'll go in the Jeep, Greaves said. The road's not real good going in.

On the way Binder tried to find out all Greaves knew about the Beales, but the real estate agent professed to know very little at all. Or any Beales either, there being none remaining in the town that had been named for them. Greaves was handling the property for a descendant in Memphis, a great-great-granddaughter who was not even named Beale anymore.

Binder rode in silence then, watching the country slip past, the ends of cornrows clocking past like spokes in a neverending wheel, fields of heat-blighted corn segueing into dusty fencerows of sumac and honeysuckle and elderberry, all talcumed alike with thick accretions of dust from the slipstreams of passing automobiles. Here and there a tidy white farmhouse tucked well back from the road in the shade of a grove of trees, a distant tractor slowmoving and noiseless, towing a great wake of white dust.

He guessed whatever had afflicted the Beales had driven them apart and ultimately scattered them like a handful of thrown stones. He didn't know what he had expected, or even what he had hoped for. A descendant, perhaps, who would tell him old stories heard at Daddy's knees. Hearthside memories you couldn't buy with gold. Old foxed papers in spidery penscrawls, journals from a pastoral corner of dementia.

The road kept branching off, steadily deteriorating until the Jeep seemed to be leaping from one raincut gully to the next, steadily ascending, the red road winding through a field promiscuous with wildflowers and goldenrod, leveling out when the cedar row began. He smelled the cedars, faintly nostalgic, the road straightening and moving between their trunks, and then in the distance he could see the house.

A great graywhite bulk looming against the greenblack of the riotous summer hills, tall and slateroofed and stately and, he thought instantly, profoundly malefic. He was suddenly of two minds about it: he wanted to flee back to Chicago and he wanted the peace he intuitively felt he could find within its walls. There was a timeless quality about it that seemed to diminish any problems he might have. In this bright moment of revelation he knew that it was less than he had expected, and incalculably more. Part log, part woodframe, part stone, it seemed to have grown at all angles like something organic turned malignant and perverse before ultimately dying, for Binder saw death in its eyes, last year's leaves in driven windrows on the front porch, two of the second-story windows stoned blind or blown out by hunters' guns. The house seemed mantled with an almost indefinable sense of dissolution, profoundly abandoned, unwanted, shunned.

Great God, Binder said.

Greaves glanced at him sharply. Been added on to a time or two, hasn't it?

Once or twice, Binder agreed. Or else they kept changing their minds while it was under construction.

Greaves stopped the Jeep. Water's down there, he said, pointing southward where beyond gray and weathered cornstalks a stream moved bright as quicksilver in the sun. That comes down from the wellhouse. Good water, he added professionally, going into his pitch. Cold as ice, it'll ache your teeth. The spring flows out of a cave on yonder hill.

Beale Cave, Binder said automatically.

That's right, Beale Cave. But if you buy it you can call it Binder Cave or whatever you want.

It surprises me that a house in that good a shape sat empty so long.

Say it does? Hell. I could show you a halfdozen others in a ten-minute drive. They ain't no work around here. And the big farmers have choked the little man right out of a livin. Folks is leavin here as they get old enough to have to work, cause there damn near ain't nothin for em to do here. Starve or git on the welfare. Get them foodstamps. And the folks that's stayin couldn't keep up no such place as that.

I guess that's right.

What do you work at?

Right now I am sort of looking for work.

Greaves produced a ring of keys large as a grapefruit, selected one, unlocked the deadbolted double doors, opened them onto a foyer the size of Binder's Chicago living room. Walls rose plumb and sheer to a dizzying height. A staircase climbed into near-dark shadows. Arched doors opened left and right, shadowy furniture crouched shapeless in shroudlike draping.

It's furnished, Binder said in surprise.

Oh yes. The furniture goes with it. It was rented as is until two years ago. Then Mrs. Lindsay decided to sell it.

You mean people lived here as recently as two years ago?

Certainly they did. Two old ladies, sisters they was. The Misses Abernathy. What did you expect? The house is a little rundown, couple of panes of glass out, but it's certainly sound as a dollar, and it's been kept up. Why does it surprise you that folks lived here?

I don't know, Binder said lamely. I thought the Beales were far-mers. This doesn't look like the sort of house a farmer would build.

The Beales were wealthy, for those times anyway. And Drewry seemed to wind up with all of it; he lived here until his death. Greaves lit a cigarette, stood for a moment cupping the dead match. Mr. Binder, you look around all you want to. I'm gonna sort of inspect the outside. See what needs painting.

All right.

Greaves turned in the doorway. You get lost just holler right loud. I'll be where I can hear you.

Cold smell of long burntout fires, hot smell of wood baking in the sun. The dry nearmetallic drone of dirtdaubers plying their craft in the hot still air. A startled bird whirring to instantaneous life at the opening of a bedroom door, flying with blind desperation into the broken glass of a window, a tinkle of glass striking stone two stories below. He looked down. Greaves in his khakis leaning against the Jeep, his round, bored face peering bemusedly up.

He saw nothing out of the ordinary, heard nothing he could not account for. He went back downstairs into the shady yard.

He told Greaves he wanted a six-month lease. Greaves shook his head. He didn't know about that.

My client wants a quick sale, he said. She hasn't said a word to me about leasing.

Well, give me an option to buy, then. If she's been wanting a quick sale for two years and you haven't gotten it yet then I don't see what six months would hurt. I'd think she'd be glad to lease.

Greaves looked pained, as if Binder had maligned his ability to sell real estate. Well, it's not that I couldn't have moved the place, Mr. Binder. It's the times. There's a recession on, money's tight, and the interest rate is higher than a cat's back.

Binder was watching him. To say nothing of the place's unsavory reputation, he said.

Greaves took off his glasses, wiped them gently with tissue he took out of his shirt pocket. Without the glasses his blue eyes looked vulnerable and defenseless. When he put them on he looked at Binder with an expression almost of amusement. Now where did you hear that, Mr. Binder? Surely not from banker Qualls?

No. Not from Mr. Qualls the banker. I read a book about this place.

Say you did? Oh, I got your number now. The famous Beale haunting. All that stuff in the eighteen hundreds. Do you mean to stand here in the cold light of day and tell me man to man that you believe any of that bullshit?

Binder just watched him, enjoying himself, imagining Greaves trying to figure out just how much he knew, amused too at the thought that the tales Greaves wanted to shield him from were the very tales that had brought him six hundred and fifty miles from Chicago, a hundred and thirty-five years too late.

You only got half my number, Binder said. I heard about the other stuff, too. He was shooting blind and in the dark here, but knew with a blood-quickening certainty that he had been right.

Greaves bit. You mean that Swaw business in the thirties? Mr. Binder, he said, looking away across the fields toward where the horizon ran, lush green folding into an austere blue of distance. You take a piece of land, any piece of land, and if a man had the longevity and the inclination to just sit and watch it for a hundred and fifty years, no telling what he'd see. You'd be surprised. People ain't never been anything else besides people and ever now and then they're going to slip up and do the same sickening things folks've been known to slip up and do before. And that don't affect the land, neither. It don't haunt it or cheapen it or wear it out. It's still the same piece of ground it was in the beginning.

I've just heard folks've seen things here. Lights and such.

There's certain folks that'll see things most anywhere. Those Abernathy women lived here from…1966 to 1978, and never seen a light or heard a rat in the walls for all I know. Anyway, the rent money come the first of ever month regular as a clock ticking.

Can you show me where the old houseplace was?

I can't today, he said, glancing at a wristwatch. I've got to show another place on Sinking Creek. But I can tell you good enough so's you can find it.

All right. Will you ask her about the lease?

I sure will, Mr. Binder. I'll do what I can. You sure you want it, ghosts and all?

He called the motel the next afternoon. The place was Binder's for six months. A bird in the hand, he figured.

Jesus, a mall, Binder said, still not quite believing it. Beale Station with a Walmart and a McDonald's and JCPenneys, a mall, everything.

Cheer up, Corrie told him, laughing, opening the car door. It's probably haunted too.

Fairy Queen of the Haunted Mall, Binder said crossing the parking lot, Stephie skipping along before them, Corrie swinging on his arm.

There was a brief magic to the day. They bought living-room drapes and kitchen curtains and a bedspread and curtains for Stephie's room. Stephie begged for not one but two videocassettes of Disney's *Adventures of Winnie the Pooh*. Binder splurged on a pair of aviator sunglasses.

To Corrie time seemed to accelerate, to move at a different pace than the time the homeplace ran on. They ate at McDonald's and saw a movie at the multiplex and suddenly the day was gone and it was time to go home.

They fell silent on the road ascending through the cedars. The house rose before them somber and still silent and imbued with the quality of patient waiting.

Everybody out, Binder said. Home sweet home.

Corrie gave him a swift callid look, as if to see was he serious or not.

Corrie had been fighting nervousness all day by staying busy. Unpacking, replacing the faded curtains with her own, trying to force her mind blank, free of anything that would make her think of her father. Alone in the house, the afternoon seemed endless. She caught herself listening for footsteps. Once she thought she heard voices that led her from room to room, listening, but ultimately there was only the moribund silence of the July day.

What could David be doing out there? she wondered. All there is is woods, how long does it take to look at a tree? She had a sudden image of David dying of snakebite. Hadn't the real estate agent specifically warned them about snakes? Copperheads always been bad on Sinking Creek, he'd said. I wouldn't feel right about my job if I didn't warn you. Specially with this little blondheaded gal here.

I could finish unpacking, she thought, seeing the cardboard boxes still stacked in the hall. But she hated the thought of it; anyway, what would she do with it? And it would just have to be repacked when they left.

David had said he would help her, and she guessed he figured he had. He had unpacked his books and put them on shelves, cleaned his typewriter and changed the ribbon and arranged it on a makeshift desk he'd constructed of two filing cabinets and an old door he found in the toolshed. With his books shelved and his workspace prepared, David felt at home anywhere.

The remaining boxes were all David's as well, except for one or two belonging to their daughter, Stephanie. Magazines. David had a peculiar reverence for the printed word that apparently forbade him throwing away anything it was printed on, so that during their marriage they had moved from apartment to apartment an ever-increasing number of boxes filled with old *Esquire*, *Playboy*, *Harper's*, battered old copies of *Ramparts* and *Rolling Stone*.

She smiled wryly at one box marked STEPHANIE.

He had apparently communicated this trait to his daughter; she was five years old and she already had her own twinebound box containing back numbers of *Children's Digest* and *Humpty Dumpty*.

The thought of Stephanie drew Corrie to the screen door. She heard the slow creak of the swing chains, saw Stephanie rocking listlessly. Stephie, as she was called, had her mother's fair skin and hair, but temperamentally she seemed closer to David: she already showed signs of being as imaginative as he was. Corrie might have said over-imaginative. Sometimes David and Stephie seemed attuned to a wider spectrum of sensory impulses than Corrie knew existed.

David taught her to read early. Her kindergarten teacher in Chicago had suspected she was gifted, and a series of tests administered to her bore this out. David reacted to the news as if he had been personally and entirely responsible. I told you so, he kept telling Corrie, as if she had maintained that the child was a congenital idiot. Or as if his genes had been transmuted to Stephie pristine and untainted by Corrie's. Though she guessed that wasn't fair; after all, it had been David who had read to her from the time he had gotten the child's attention, and at a period in his life when time had been at a premium.

She opened the door and went out onto the porch. Stephie sat idly turning the pages of a book about gnomes, but she was no longer looking at them with any semblance of interest.

She looked up at Corrie. Can we watch TV?

No, we can't. Sorry.

Why not?

Daddy didn't hook it up to the antenna yet.

David had said that he would, but Corrie had turned it on a little past noon and there was only the blank white screen, the white noise of static emanating from the speaker. The lead wire wasn't even hooked to the little screws on the back of the set, and when she finally found a screwdriver and leant over the set to fix it she had seen through the window the antenna itself leaned against the back porch wall, still in its cardboard carton. Maybe he would tomorrow. Or tonight, if he came in in time.

Corrie had left the sound on anyway, turned all the way up. At least it was something out of this century. Nothing else in the house seemed to be.

Don't you want to play in the playhouse Daddy fixed you?

She closed the book. I suppose so, she said. She arose and went somewhat grudgingly down the flagstone steps toward the playhouse under the elm. She played as if it were work she was forced to do, Corrie thought, thinking of herself. Today she had felt like a child forced to play grownup in a cavernous nineteenth-century house with someone else's furniture, someone else's past.

Though not forced, she thought hastily. David had been scrupulously fair about that. It had been a joint decision. Except that David had thought of it, David had been the one enthused about it, and David had a way of leading you along on the ragged edge of his enthusiasm until you were someplace you hadn't planned to be, wondering how you got there. She could have gone to Orlando and stayed with her older sister Ruthie and her husband Vern; she could have stayed in Chicago. But she knew that David would have done it anyway. He would have come alone, and that would have been worse.

David had been a drifter when he married her, and though he had made an enormous effort to change or at least convince her he had changed, there was still a lot of drifter in him: a refusal to put down roots, to think of any one place as home, a disinclination to do for very long anything he didn't want to do. He just wouldn't be bored. There was no pretense of politeness about him. She had heard him kill a hundred boring conversations just by shutting up.

A goddamned hippie, her father (her father: the word fell through her mind like a stone settling slowly through deep water) had called him contemptuously. Among other things, a lot worse. Those had been hard times, when she and her father had both said ugly unforgivable things to each other, things that still rang in her ears. She had always been her father's favorite, and suddenly a gulf had opened between them she couldn't close. She hadn't had an excuse for the things she had said, though her father had the best one in the world: he was dying of an undiagnosed brain tumor, was already dying the moment she accused him of just going crazy and mean.

Even as she tried to think of David, another level of her mind twisted in guilty pain and she realized how much she missed her father. Grief cut her clean and deep as a surgeon's scalpel, and in that moment she would have clawed the dirt from his casket to see his face.

She forced herself to quit thinking about that, to make her mind gray and blank as the television screen she was watching. But it wouldn't completely go away, and a part of it wondered detachedly how much would he have decayed, would I know him, could I stand to touch him.

She forced her mind, by a sheer exertion of will, to forsake her father's face, to think of David. She seemed to have known him forever. He was five years older than Corrie, but in certain respects a generation apart. In 1968, when he had been listening to Bob Dylan, she had been thirteen. There were fundamental differences that showed even in so insignificant a thing as the music they liked: he still played Dylan and the Stones, she liked middle-of-the-road and country, neither of which David could tolerate. He said it was junk, Muzak, throwaway plastic. He said Dylan was a poet, that if he hadn't grown up in an electronic society Dylan would have been writing his apocalyptic visions for the little magazines, and he heard dark and sinister undercurrents in the music of the Rolling Stones that she just didn't hear.

She was like her father: fiscally responsible, possessed of a healthy respect for the dollar. David simply didn't care, though she guessed that was changing. Ever since they'd learned she was pregnant again, David seemed to think about nothing but ways to make money. He had been just as happy broke as he was when he had money. When he came back from Vietnam, he was discharged in California and blew his mustering outpay on a typewriter and a Suzuki motorcycle, which she had never even seen. He had wrecked it in Tempe, Arizona, only one state out of California, and had just walked off and left it.

The word Vietnam had dark connotations for Corrie, like a spectre watching over their shoulders. She blamed it for the changes in David. She had been thirteen when he left for his tour of duty, and up until then he had never spoken a dozen words to her in her life. She barely knew him. He was cleancut, a little reserved maybe, but the image of the boy next door. When she saw him four years later he looked...not exactly grubby, but not exactly the boy next door anymore. His hair was long, not shoulderlength or anything, but long, and he had a beard. But the worst thing was his eyes. They had changed, looked at you cold and impassively out of the dark beard-shadowed face, as if nothing much mattered to them one way or another.

There was a strong air of single-minded purpose about him, too much intensity: you couldn't call him laid back. She really believed he could do anything he wanted to do. Even for a while when he had long hair and a beard and had gone about in old Army fatigues he had always known who he was, what he was, what to do about it.

He was a writer. Even then he had been writing stories and sending them away and getting them back along with the little impersonal rejection slips. But Corrie saw that David had known he was a writer; he was just waiting for the world to catch up, which it finally had, in Chicago.

He's not much fun, is he? Ruthie had said before they were married. Ruthie had tried to seduce him, she guessed. David never said so, but Ruthie always tried to seduce everybody at some time or other, especially Corrie's boyfriends. And the occasional man who didn't succumb she dismissed as being no fun anyway.

Actually he had been quite a bit of fun. He could be charming when he wanted to, and he had wanted to quite frequently then, when they were going together, getting engaged, when things weren't pushing at him so.

He could be persuasive, too. He had made love to her the first night she had gone out with him. She had been a virgin, couldn't quite figure how it happened, and the next day she was assailed with guilt, not at the loss of some intangible something she had never been aware of possessing but at the idea that she had been so easy and at the thought that David would think her cheap. She was angry at herself, and a little puzzled. Why had she let him when she wouldn't let anyone else?

It took her a while to see that she had done it simply because he had wanted her too. He had wanted her with the focused intensity he applied to all the things he wanted. No one else had wanted her that intensely. He had just assumed she was going to let him, and she had.

The descending twilight was hot and still. A blood sun of eventide. Silence save the sleeping droning of insects, the spill of water over the shelf of limestone. The rabbit came up out of the thick ferment of wild peppermint by the springhouse and leapt nimbly stone to stone across the damp dark loam. The air here was cool and it smelled richly of mint.

The rabbit went up the path that bordered the creek. It paused crossing a sandbar where a water moccasin lay curled. The snake stirred, somnolent eyes becoming alert, its entire attention focused on the rabbit. The rabbit gave no indication of fear. It watched the snake levelly with its black shoebutton eyes. The snake seemed to sense something amiss: it abruptly slithered up the branch, dropped with a splash into the creek, fled across the water in a series of S-shaped undulations.

The rabbit turned. She was a young rabbit, halfgrown perhaps, lean and stringybodied. She went up the embankment, feet scuttling in the sand, came out into a field of red clover. The clover was in bloom and the air was filled with droning bees and the red clover perfume but the rabbit did not pause to feed. She skirted the darker side of the field and went through a thick hedgerow grown up over a splitrail fence. She came up through the garden spot, watching the house. Her nose crinkled delicately as she scented the air.

She was watching the girl. The girl was playing under the dark of a beech tree.

———

Stephie came slowly up the steps, stopped and sat down on the porch. She looked out toward the toolshed at the lower edge of the yard, upward and beyond it to the green and umber sedgefield rising to meet the dark line of trees. Corrie knew she was looking for David. He had been ascending the ridge when Stephie had seen him last.

When is Daddy coming in? I'm hungry.

I don't know. When he comes.

What does that mean, when he comes?

It just means your father does things the way he wants to and when he wants to.

Is that a good way to be?

Corrie paused. The child was watching her with calm, level eyes. Impersonal as a tape recorder, Corrie thought against her will. But this sounded like one of Stephie's loaded questions: she seemed almost hypersensitive to any criticism that David might receive.

I suppose it is if you can do it. Some people can't. I can't, and sometimes when people do that kind of thing it makes it hard on other people.

Why is he hunting for a place an old house used to be?

Your daddy is writing a book. Sometimes he acts peculiar when he's busy doing that. He…he gets involved with what he's writing about.

I'm going to be a writer.

Corrie knew that Stephanie was sometimes disquieting to other people, especially when they listened to their conversations. They didn't quite know how to talk to her, never knew what she knew and what she didn't. Sometimes her friends had treated Stephanie as if she were afflicted with a disease with a high mortality rate instead of merely being precocious; Corrie herself thought of them as a family comprised of three adults, two regular-sized and one trial-sized.

And one on the way, she thought, a twinge of unfocused worry flickering through her.

He came onto the place with an air of discovery, an archeologist seeking the chaos of an older time. He hunkered in the windy sedge at the rim of the hill and examined it. He could see how the old homeplace and yard below him were set in the epicenter of a saucerlike depression in the earth perhaps a half mile in diameter, the house set at the end of a dual lane of cedars that flanked the drive, down which ran droves of curiosity-seekers to hear spectral voices and obscene babbling, watch phantom figures and lights drift about the fields. According to contemporary accounts, few came away disappointed. Binder didn't plan on being disappointed either. He felt a growing obsession to unstring the secrets the house held, to unravel the Gordian knot time and myth had only tightened.

Where the house had stood was a tangle of riotous weeds and brush, the twin chimneys rising starkly out of the undergrowth. It was caught in the slow sweep of failing light, the sky beyond it redorange and metallic, flooded with garish colors as if all the light in the world had pooled there, congesting momentarily at the horizon and then draining off the rim of the world. Struck by the gradations of light and shadow Binder watched in an almost rapt stillness the subtle changes the shifting light brought, objects altering slowly as if undergoing some metamorphosis at their core, their very cells being rearranged. Though he was not an artist he studied the scene with the intensity of a painter, eyes marking color and shading, the tilt of the sedge, the darkening and accruing shadows seemingly drawn out of the earth itself.

He was watching the homeplace and he was pondering the nature of its evil, not wondering if there was evil indeed there but knowing it with an absolute certainty that he applied to very few things. What triggered it? he wondered. How did it work? And how did it ever come to be there? Something old and evil had happened here, so evil that everything that had come after was just echoes, just spreading ripples in the water so intense that Beale and his family had ultimately abandoned the house and rebuilt in the place he was now moving into. Though that didn't help, did it, Old Jake? Binder thought. Whatever it was just walked across the ridge and knocked at your door.

Binder had seen old pictures where the house itself looked ungainly and out of proportion, the original log structure added to with seemingly with no eye for symmetry or even common sense, so that ultimately the house took on an air of inherent arrogance or just the unmindful disconcern of the very old, serene, and timeless.

There was, he saw again, juxtaposition of lineament that jarred him. No angle seemed to be true to the eye's expectation. The horizontal seemed slightly out of level, the vertical just a fraction out of plumb. Perhaps this very imbalance lay at the root of things; an eye perpetually beguiled and a brain constantly reevaluating these images might draw insanity to it like a comforter. Yet he knew the evil predated the house, and he looked farther to the land itself, the sedgefield running stonily down the hill to the outbuildings, to what must have been the carriage house, and far beyond that, the ruins of the slave cabins.

It was an evil perhaps indigenous to the slope and rise of the land, to the stark austerity of the woods surrounding the ruined plantation. For whatever course, it was a verifiable fact that evil had happened here. He had the book, the old newspapers. Such word-of-mouth stories as he had been able to collect. Arcs had fallen here, and fallen again. Blood had run like the proverbial water. And before that, in the nineteenth century, the homeplace had been the setting for a sort of pastoral haunting so bizarre and irrefutable that word of mouth and finally an article in so prestigious a source as the *Saturday Evening Post* had drawn the curious hordes to listen for voices in the night whispers, to see Casper candles flit about the fields.

He had come equipped to unravel it all, to line the yellow sheets of foolscap with the place's true history. It was a book he was compelled to write. By what? His interest, the writer's interest, by some misalignment of his consciousness. What was his fault, how had it picked him?

Or had he picked it?

On the way back he passed through the old graveyard. Abandoned by the living, only the dead kept their watch. He sat down on one of the headstones. After a while he arose and started back, stopping for a moment at Jacob Beale's headstone. It seemed imbued with lost knowledge, secrets carried to the grave, deadbolts he could open could he just find the right sequence of numbers.

JACOB WILLIAM BEALE 1785 ~ 1844

TORTURED BY A SPIRIT, NOW AT REST

ORIGINAL STONE STOLEN IN 1937, THIS ROCK PLACED IN 1941

He didn't linger here. He had seen it before and it held nothing new for him.

It was a scant two hundred yards over the sedgefield and down the ridge to the house. Here he stopped again, studying the place. There was a look of great age about it. Save the anomolaic four-wheel-drive truck parked in the yard, he could have stepped backward into the middle of the previous century.

Behind Binder the field sloped continually upward in a stony tapestry of sedge and faded into a blue wood. That was where the old woman watched him from blueberry eyes in the warm, quilted leather of her face. Her hair was black without a streak of gray and frizzed out from beneath the man's felt hat jammed on her head. She wore walking shoes and a shapeless pair of men's corduroy pants and a gray sweater whose buttons were split away and she had clasped the front with safety pins. She was old, but she looked wiry and tough, as if her bones had been strung on rawhide thongs and her skin tanned to leather. Her hands were big-knuckled and large as a man's.

One of these hands clasped the wadded mouth of a gunny sack. Something stirred in it. She lowered the weight to the ground to rest her arm, still watching the distant figure of the man, thinking, Well there you are, sure enough. Reckon how long you'll be here? She released her grip on the sack momentarily. As if sensing this tentative freedom, whatever was in the bag leapt spasmodically against the restraining burlap, but she stayed it with a foot and went back to watching him. The bag stilled.

Just like a man, she thought. Look for an hour when there's nothing in the world to see. You needn't go lookin for it anyway, she told Binder's angular figure. When it gits ready for you it'll come huntin you up.

Her shadow had lengthened, she felt the lessening of the sun's weight. She took up the bag and slung it across a shoulder. She would have liked to have watched the man longer but she did not want to be on the Beale farm after dark, and besides, the woods were full of dead treetops where logs had been cut and hauled away and they lay like deadfalls awaiting tripping. So at length she turned toward deeper woods, came out in a clearing above which a hawk wheeled, fleeing the raucous tormenting of a flock of crows. She stopped to watch. The hawk ascended into a darkening void, vanished. A whippoorwill called from the shadowed wood and she went on.

Below him the lights came on. The door opened and a rectangle of yellow spilled onto the yard. He could see Corrie, doll-size, approaching the steps, peering into the gathering night. He could imagine her face sweetly becoming slightly apprehensive as night drew on. Afraid of the dark, he thought derisively, who would have welcomed anything the night might choose to favor him with.

David, David.

He could hear her calling, the voice belllike yet faint with distance. He arose and took up his notebook, went stumbling blindly downhill toward the lighted house.

You were out a long time, Corrie said.

She thought you were snakebit, Stephanie told David.

My name is Mommy, Corrie said. Not she.

Binder laid aside his silverware, took up his coffee cup. I finally found the old Beale homeplace, he said. Greaves said it would be easy, and maybe in the wintertime it would, but this place is so grown up you can't find anything. I fought blackberry briars all afternoon and finally just stumbled upon it. The two chimneys are there, just like Greaves said, but he neglected to mention there are trees growing right up beside them, taller than they are. Right up through where the floor of the house was, poplars forty or fifty feet tall. I keep forgetting this was all a hundred and forty years ago.

What else was there?

The pear tree old Jacob Beale set out in his yard. Dead, I'll admit, but a pear tree nonetheless. The graveyard where the Beales are buried. The old orchard. You can see the configuration of the land, the lay of it, where the fields were, the old grape arbor. The spring is still there, of course, and the wreckage of the old stone springhouse.

A regular scenic tour, she said, smiling wryly.

What amazes me is that we got here while there was anything at all left...I expected to find everything razed, the ground bulldozed, house trailers setting everywhere.

He waited for her to echo his enthusiasm but she did not. She arose and began to clear the table. Binder lit a cigarette, glancing outside. The windows had gone opaque, dark stolen over the land. He could see his reflected image at the head of the table, the shadow of a beard he was beginning to grow blurring the edges of his face. Lit bright orange by the flare of the match, his reflection was oblique and conspiratorial.

How long do you think it will take you to block out the book? Do you think you can get the feel of it here—begin it, maybe— and then we could go back to Chicago to finish it?

I don't know, Corrie. It'll just come when it comes. Why? I don't recall you being that fond of Chicago.

I wasn't, but I'm not that fond of the Beale farm, either. This place, especially this old house, just drives me up the wall. Besides, there's school to think about.

This is only July. There's plenty of time to think about that. It'll all be worth it, Corrie. I promise you.

Well. I hope it's a good book.

I don't know how good it'll be but it'll be commercial. And that's what this is all about, isn't it?

I suppose so. I know you can write. You don't have to prove anything to me, David.

When the house had been modernized, a bathroom had been added in the largest downstairs bedroom, a partition erected so there was a narrow hall that ended in two doors, one to the bathroom, the other interconnecting with a smaller bedroom. They had bought Stephie bunk beds in Beale Station. Corrie had set them up in the smaller room and done what she could to brighten it up, but the walls were a drab dirty brown and the room still had the austere appearance of a dormitory or military barracks.

Or prison, she thought.

Binder read to Stephie until he thought she slept, then ceased. She lay with her eyes closed for a time, but when he softly closed the book and arose to leave she opened them. When she spoke her voice was blurred with sleep.

Daddy?

What?

I forgot to tell you about the lady I saw.

Lady? Where did you see a lady, babe?

Stephie had arisen on her elbows. Her face was animated now, no longer sleepy. Binder thought she looked like a tiny clone of her mother.

On the hill above the toolshed. She had something. A rabbit, I think. It kept trying to get away but she held it real tight and it didn't.

A rabbit? Binder thought. Aloud he said, What did the lady look like, Stephie? Did she look like anybody we know?

No, she was real old. Sort of fat and mean-looking. Grouchy.

Where did she go?

I don't know. Just away. The way you went. She...she shook her hand at me.

You mean she waved? Or what?

Sort of…she waved her hand but it wasn't fingers. Her fingers didn't wave.

Shook her fist? he wondered. At a child?

Her eyelids fluttered. He could see sleep rising up in her blue eyes like a soft mist. It was a brown rabbit, she said drowsily. Then she fell silent.

He sat beside the bed, waiting until she was sound asleep. Sometimes she pretended, letting him get all the way to the door, then calling, Daddy…

He was thinking about rabbits. Something about rabbits. Then he remembered the man the real estate agent had sent to clear the place of weeds and brush. He and Stephie had been watching the red tractor moving through the lawless growth of pigweed and sassafras and all at once there was a hellacious noise beneath the blade of the bush hog. The driver got off swearing, kicking through the weeds to find the stump he had hit. But there was no stump. He approached Binder with a curious look on his face.

Hope that wadn't you or your little girl's rabbit box, he said.

Go in the house, he told Stephie.

I want to see the rabbits, she said stubbornly.

I said go in the house. Tell Mommy I said to give you some ice cream.

Binder went to see. The operator had raised the mower. Beneath it, shattered, they saw dowels and lashes of wood, a near-unidentifiable wreckage of splinters.

You can't prove to me that ever was a rabbit box, he said. But the weeds were showered with bright drops of blood, sticky bits of hair and flesh and white shards of bone, as if some furry creature had exploded all over the lawn.

I'll keep this to myself, Binder thought. It wasn't the sort of thing he wanted Corrie to know, high-strung as she was, and with her father dying...if Stephie hadn't told her already.

Did you tell Mommy about seeing the lady? he asked. But this time she really was asleep.

Corrie sat in silence for a time, a prolonged silence that Binder had come to recognize. It meant that Corrie was going to ask him something she knew he'd rather not be asked.

David?

What? Binder was holding his notebook but he wasn't working. He was waiting.

You think it would bother you if Ruthie and Vern came up for a few days sometime this summer?

I guess not, he said reluctantly, mildly annoyed but at the same time realizing that he couldn't deny her so simple a request. He planned to be deep in the book all summer and to have little time for small talk. Vern was very big on small talk.

Vern was successful. He had once been a construction worker, a few years ago, and had fallen from a rigging of scaffold. Binder had once maintained, not entirely facetiously, that Vern had jumped in order to sue the company. He had won an enormous lawsuit, had even been rolled into the courtroom in a wheelchair. The money was no more than in his hands than Vern was healed by a traveling evangelist in a miracle bright and incandescent that Binder figured was probably the peak of the faith healer's career. Vern and Ruthie had immediately moved to Florida and gone into the motel business.

Vern didn't like Binder. In fact he probably didn't like Binder almost as much as Binder didn't like him. Vern didn't trust anyone who didn't have a job or wasn't rich; he felt if you weren't filthy rich you ought to be punching a timeclock somewhere. He had never really understood what it was that Binder did. The idea that a grown man would spend his time writing made-up stories in a notebook amazed him, and the idea that there were folks in New York who would pay Binder for this was simply beyond his comprehension.

I don't care if they come, it'll be company for you and Stephie and God knows there's enough room. But Vern'll have to find his own games to play. I'll be busy then and he needn't look to me for entertainment.

I told them you'd be working. I'll be glad to see Ruthie again, though. It seems we never see each other anymore except when there's trouble in the family. Ruthie worries about me. You know how big sisters are.

No, I don't. When did this plan come about, anyway?

After Daddy's…when Daddy died.

She had crossed the room, came up behind him where he sat. He felt her hands alighting on his shoulders, saw in the mirrored windows their reflections merge. She leant her face to the top of his head, her hair so fair against his own. He could smell her hair.

Poor, lonely David. You were an only child when I found you.

He smiled at her reflection. I was an only child before that. You want something else, I can tell. What?

Fix the TV so it works tomorrow?

All right.

It'll liven up the place some.

He was silent a time. Look, he finally said. I don't want you thinking I've dragged you into something against your will. I'm only here to write the book. And I've always wanted to see this place, and this seemed like a good chance to do it. You could have stayed in Chicago. Or Orlando.

No. I wanted to be with you.

We could stay nights in a motel, then. If the house upsets you that much, I mean.

No. That would be crazy, even if we could afford it. It'll be all right, David. Really. You're committed to do the book, and that's the important thing right now.

His silence bespoke assent but he already knew better, had known from his first night here, from before that. From the day he had come here with Greaves, the night he had read the book in Chicago. The book he was writing was important to him, but it was becoming secondary to the mystery. All the things that were supposed to have gone on down here: had they or hadn't they? Had all those people lied? It was over a century ago, layered with myth and folklore, but what was the basis of it? He felt he had the pieces to an enormously complex puzzle, needed only time to figure out where they went.

Night. She slept, or perhaps she feigned sleep. Lately he thought that she sometimes did. He could feel her regular breathing against his back. He couldn't hear the sounds outside the bedroom window, only the mesmeric whirring of the fan. The fan negated the heat, the whippoorwills, created an artificial environment of no sound no climate no time that Corrie needed to induce sleep.

The first day in the house it hadn't occurred to them the place wasn't air conditioned, and that night they had lain sleepless and sweaty in the dark. The next day he went to Beale Station and bought a fan to use until the air conditioner was installed.

Binder had told himself that he could sleep anywhere, but he couldn't tonight. His mind seemed wired on adrenaline, his eyes kept opening to stare upward at the unseen ceiling, and when he tried to clear his mind, to be completely blank, scenes from the book he was beginning flickered across it bright and chaotic as snippets of colored film.

It had to work. Too much riding on it, too many things. Lying there in the dark, he itemized them in his mind like a man going over things he had bought on credit and wondering how he was going to pay for them.

The money. All his money—Corrie's money, really, but what's mine is yours—thrown into the pot for a single quixotic toss of the dice. All right. Six-month lease, eighteen hundred dollars. Twenty-four hundred for a used pickup truck. Four hundred to an obstetrician, and more to come there. Utility bills. Food for twenty-four weeks at...seventy-five? Ninety-five hundred dollars to start with.

He thought of Stephie. Of the nameless and faceless child in Corrie's womb. How could Corrie have let him do this? How could she have stood by and calmly watched him put all her hard-won eggs in one basket?

Well, to start with, she didn't know about the location of all the eggs. He expected she believed that a great many of them still resided at the Blount County bank.

Her sleeping body stirred against him and he felt a rush of love for her. He needed her. He needed her practicality, her intense concern for the mundane minutiae of the world he wouldn't or couldn't cope with. He even needed her faint ridicule; it sharpened him, kept him moving, let him know when he was drifting too close to the edge that had always fascinated him. Yet a part of his mind stood apart, detached and uninvolved, and asked him how much he would love her if there ever came a time when he didn't need her.

The book had thrown her off balance. She hadn't expected the money, the good reviews, the award it received. He could imagine her drawing back, regrouping, confused, thinking, Well, maybe he knows what he's doing after all. Maybe I ought to give him more rope. Maybe he won't hang himself.

Her hips moved against his thigh and he wondered what she was dreaming. He smiled wryly into the darkness. Your mind is as cold as a cat's heart, but your body didn't get the news.

How much could he realistically expect? Fifteen thousand? Twenty? If the book went over there might be a film sale...

He got up furtively and pulled on his pants. He took up his lighter and cigarettes and went out of the dark bedroom through the high-ceilinged foyer to the porch. The door was open save a screen and a cool breeze blew off the creek. He opened the screen and went out into the sounds of the summer night. He sat on the top step smoking and listening to the crying of the crickets and the lonesome call of an owl from somewhere out there in the far-off darkness.

Here in the moonlight the world seemed drained of color. The outlines of objects took on an added clarity, as if their edges had been sketched in charcoal. For no reason he could name he found himself watching the old toolshed, a leaning structure of gray planking set against the base of the hill. Above it the hill undulated eastward, cold and silverlooking in the moonlight, broken only by the dark stains of cedars. He found himself waiting, staring intently at the doorway of the toolshed, a rectangle of Cimmerian darkness that seemed beyond darkness, darkness multiplied by itself, and he was thinking, Something is going to happen. He sensed a change in the air. It had grown denser yet, so that even the crying of the nightbirds could not pierce it. He seemed locked in a void of silence. The crickets had ceased or the roaring in his ears diminished them. He had fallen into a helpless, volitionless state, no longer a participant but an observer, a person things happen to, straining to see he knew not what but watching with rapt fascination an oblong abscission into warm, mustysmelling darkness.

He became conscious of a painful constriction of his chest and realized suddenly that he had been holding his breath. The cigarette burned his fingers. He looked down when he put out the cigarette and when he looked up he could hear the nightbirds again and the toolshed had lost its air of dark menace. It was only a shakeroofed outbuilding collapsing infinitesimally slowly under its own weight.

He felt chilled and shaky. All right, he told the house. We both know you can do it. You don't have to prove anything to me.

The roof was already hot to the touch at eight a.m. and by nine he could feel slick trails of sweat across his ribcage and down his back. The white shirt was plastered across his shoulder blades, and after a while he took it off and balled it in his fist and tossed it off the edge of the roof.

He moved carefully toward the ridge of the house, balancing the antenna and pole and watching his tennis-shoed feet, careful of their placement. Some of the slates were loose, earlier one had skittered beneath a foot and fallen to the concrete patio below, a dizzying distance from the apex of the roof.

There was no way to secure anything on the slate roof, and eventually he settled for leaning the antenna pole against one of the chimneys and securing it with wire. When he released it the pole skewed sideways with the antenna pointed toward the earth. No signal there, Binder knew, and he stood for a moment gazing up the sheer plumb side of the brick flue. No purchase for hands or feet. No thought when it was built one hundred and twenty years ago of handholds for Binder to climb, nothing to lash an antenna to. He squatted and went crablike down the roof to the edge and down the ladder to the kitchen roof, another ladder to the ground. In a few minutes he returned with a stepladder and a length of clothesline wire.

He balanced the ladder and climbed it with painstaking care, fingertips almost prehensile against the brick, a dizzy fear of heights knotted in the pit of his stomach, freshets of nervous perspiration starting from seemingly every pore.

The top. His breath whistling in his throat, he locked his hands over the lip of the chimney, feeling a heady rush of relief in a world of intangibles. Here was something a man could cling to. A rock in all this tumult. He shifted his weight, leant out over space, reaching with his right hand for the antenna, his left clinging to the top of the chimney. Then the century-old mortar gave and the brick came away in his hand, the ladder kicking out beneath him, Binder hitting the roof hard and fighting to keep consciousness, everything a dervish of movement washed in red haze. Hitting the slate on his back then and rolling, fingers clawing for purchase at the very air, grasping the antenna wire desperately and feeling it tauten momentarily and come away from the antenna with a rush of relief in his hands and his descent accelerate, heard the antenna crash to the roof somewhere above him, the elements skirting against the roof. He was grasping at the slate, tearing at it with his nails, after what seemed like hours slowing his descent and ending near the eave, every muscle of his body taut and the fingers of both hands hooked over the rough edges of a tier of slate. His head and his fingertips hurt. The world looked filtered through a red miasma of fear and anger at his own stupidity. He could feel blood soaking through the hair on his right temple, see it trickle down the index and second finger on his left hand.

David? She was calling him from somewhere below him, out of sight beneath the eaves.

He lay with his face against the roof, unmindful of the hot slate burning his cheek.

David. David.

He closed his eyes. What?

Something happened to the picture, she said.

No shit, Binder said to himself. He didn't say anything aloud.

The TV was showing a fairly plain picture then it all went away and there was nothing but snow. It's not even talking.

Did it show me going ass over kneecaps off a ladder before it all went away? he asked her.

What?

Nothing.

Are you all right, David?

Yes. I'm all right.

He guessed he was. He got up slowly, still holding on with his hands. The world turned like a stone-drunk carousel. He looked at his fingertips. The nails were bleeding. He felt for a handkerchief but didn't have one, remembered tossing the shirt off the roof. He wiped the blood off his temple with his forearm, a slick smear of bright scarlet.

He ascended the roof once more, unwired the antenna pole, and knotted the lead wire around the leg of the antenna. He began to pay out wire, lowering the antenna toward the eave of the roof.

Get out of the way, Corrie. I'm lowering it down.

What?

Just get out of the way.

The antenna tipped over the side. He braced his knees against the ridge of the roof to absorb the onset of gravity, let the wire slide through his palms until he felt the antenna settle onto solid ground. He threw the wire and it slithered away, vaguely serpentine, and vanished. He wiped the blood out of his eyes again and sat for a moment breathing hard, trying to get his bearings. He felt vague and dislocated. He hungered for the normality of fifteen minutes ago with an urgency that bordered on panic.

Naked to the waist with a white cloth tied around his longish hair, he looked vaguely like a refugee from the sixties, aging flower child disenfranchised and purposeless in 1980. He climbed the steep embankment the house seemed shored up against and through the sedge toward a flat knoll with the antenna balanced across a shoulder, reeling out line as he went.

She watched from the back porch, fretfully solicitous. A touch of concern in her voice when she called. David, it doesn't matter about the TV, really, can't you just let it go?

No, he said. If you want to see *The Tonight Show* then you'll damn well see it. Just keep the wire unreeling.

He followed a rockchoked red gully, looking over the rim of the hot metallic sky, past the worn, faded timber of the sedge. He clambered out of the gully, hoping the reel of wire he'd bought would be enough, skirting last year's cornfield. Binder wondered vaguely who had tended it, guessed the land had been rented on shares. Yet it might have been years old. The stalks were tilted and bleached to a delicate silvergray, seemed composed of some material of awesome complexity. The thin, paperlike blades hung sere and still in the windless day.

He leaned the antenna pole against a shelf of limestone protruding from the red clay and stepped up, then leapt involuntarily backward, suddenly aware of swift movement, coppercolored and nearliquid. A snake big as his forearm flowed across the smooth limestone, its skin rippling. The snake turned, halfcoiled, and for a moment Binder was staring into its deadlooking eyes, the head flattened and poised.

He looked about for a weapon, a rock small enough to throw. Go on, goddamn you, he said. I didn't set out to kill you. You never did anything to me. The snake watched him hypnotically, eyes like shards chipped off black glass, old and evil and implacable. He had a momentary vision of Corrie's tanned leg striding through the sedge, a movement too swift for the eye to follow, twin drops of scarlet beading on her calf. He slowly took up the aluminum antenna pole, smashed the end of it onto the snake's head, its four-foot length instantaneously constricting into a writhing mass of flesh, convulsing in silent agony.

He raised the pole. The snake's mouth was open, the jaws unhinged, the fangs delicate hypodermics like sharp-curved fish bones. He lowered it deliberately, smeared the snake's head across the stone. He leant, watching the snake for movement, the pole poised, pale pinkish stains on the white rock. The snake was very still.

He felt watched. He turned. Some faint noise, perhaps a whisper of wind in the dry cornstalks. A black dog watched him stoically from the edge of the cornfield. An enormous dog, high-shouldered and lean, standing cold and still as ice. He felt lost in the raw beast. The oversized, erect ears looked like a photograph he'd seen of jackals or wild African hunting dogs, the muzzle long and snoutlike, slightly open. He could see quite clearly the row of teeth and the red-looking tongue bisected dark by a shadow. Get, he told it uncertainly. Get the fuck away from here. Nothing. He looked about for a stone or a stick and saw horrified out of the tail of his eye the dog vanish. It seemed to step abruptly sidewise and become for an instant the right half of a black dog, Binder whirling to see it vanish completely, not as if it were fading out but simply stepping behind something. But there was nothing to step behind. Through the gone half of the dog he could see the motionless corn blades, the rampant growth of morning glories, the crowlike convolutions of the parched earth contrasted against the corporeal and inarguably real-looking shorthaired half of the dog. In an instant, an eyesblink, it was gone too.

He came closer. He studied the spot intently, leant for a moment openmouthed and foolish, halfcomic in profound scrutiny of the fissured clay.

He went on up the slope with the antenna and hurriedly set it up, hooking the leadwire to it abstractedly and occasionally glancing back over his shoulder at the cornfield. He lashed the pole to a fencepost with a length of wire, angled the antenna toward where he guessed Nashville was.

The cornfield seemed darker toward its center. Light entered at the rows' end, ran like liquid down the middles, getting shallower and shallower. There seemed at the convergence of the rows some mass of shadows light could not defray. He clipped the wire with the sidecutters and pocketed them and started toward the cornfield. He stopped at the spot the dog had been. He stepped into the field a few feet, the cornblades whispering against his jeans. Then he turned and went back to the house.

The TV was couched in the corner by the window, its screen flickering the particolored images of a game show, and Binder watched it, feeling a curious sense of triumph as if the television and he had been locked in combat, as if it had been some recalcitrant beast he had had to force to do his bidding.

Lunch was soup and deviled eggs and tuna fish sandwiches. Binder set across from Corrie and drank iced coffee. His head ached and he wasn't hungry. He felt slightly nauseated and sore- ness seemed to be creeping up on him like polluted water seeping from his bones.

He sat the glass down. I saw a dog out there in the cornfield, he told her.

A dog, she said, and he realized suddenly the enormity of the gap between what he had seen and what she had said. There seemed a vast gulf of windy space between the words and the still, dark beast watching him so calmly. He remembered that he hadn't seen the feet and that it had dull yellow eyes.

Probably homeless, she said musingly. A stray somebody dropped here? We ought to put out something for it to eat.

His hand faltered halfway to his mouth with the glass of coffee. For a moment he thought he might say something, then he thought better of it and didn't.

The air conditioning man had come that day, an efficient, swarthy little fellow not given to conversation. Though Corrie had certainly tried, Binder thought, half smiling in the dark, remembering her bringing him iced tea and offering sandwiches, apparently del- ighted at seeing any strange face and reacting to the sight of the red and white truck winding toward them through the cedar rows as if it were the arrival of some long and eagerly awaited visitor. The old man shifted his cud of Beech-Nut and watched her with wary little berrylike eyes, as if she were bearing suspect intentions along with mintsmelling tea.

You won't never cool it, the man told Binder. Your best bet is to shut off some of them upstairs rooms. You won't cool it this summer nor heat it this winter, not unless you're a millionaire. Cost you four, maybe five hundred a month, and them fireplaces'd keep you humpin with a chainsaw.

We'll be back in Chicago this winter, Corrie had said. This place is depressing enough in the summer. Can you imagine what it'd be like in the wintertime?

Lying there in the dark, under the cool, mechanical whine of the air conditioner, Binder thought he could. Already remote, the place shrouded with snow would be inaccessible, locked in silent peace. No telephone, no traffic, no gossip, just the quiet walls and the unlined yellow paper and time settling slowly over him like motes of dust spinning in the air.

He couldn't sleep. His head ached, the pain coming in waves so regular he could have charted them, ebbing and flowing like the black tides of the sea. And that was the way he came to see them, the waves beginning far out and uneven beyond a reef of slick black rocks starting in, whitecapping, breaking on the rocks with fingers of salty spray. Fading thin, but never completely going away. There was always a dull aching behind his eyes. He opened them, stared into the darkness. He could feel her naked back against him. His arm encircled her as if he could draw furtive comfort from her sleeping warmth. He cupped a breast gently, slid his hand down to the smooth mound of her belly, her waist already thickening in pregnancy. He thought simultaneously of the tiny form growing inside her (cells dividing even as she slept, no rest for the weary, a woman's work is never done) and the book growing on lined sheets of yellow paper and in his head. We shall each be creative, each in our own way.

He arose, went to check on Stephie, studied her sleeping face for a time. He went into the kitchen. In a cabinet he found a bottle of extra-strength Tylenol, took three with a glass of icewater from the refrigerator, stood for a moment with the cold glass against his temple.

He sat on the sofa smoking, watching the television with the sound off. Late-night news, talking heads like prophets gifted with hindsight mouthing dark forebodings intercut with neon images of random violence.

On the porch it was cooler, a degree of comfort between the sterile manufactured cold of the bedroom and the hot heavy air in the den. He sat on the damp stone steps, watching across the dark bottomland to where the horizon met the sky in a collusion of black he suspected more than saw. Distant lightning flickered there, vague and threatless, and he caught himself waiting for thunder that wouldn't come. Orange electricity bloomed and faded, burnishing the silver clouds, tracing their outlines with bright neon fire, the afterimage burning on his retinas. Beyond the toolshed the sky was black and wetlooking, velvet drowning slowly in India ink.

He talked to folks.

He took a seat on a worn bench on the courthouse square, next to an old felthatted man whetting a knife. Occasionally the man would cease his work and inspect it critically, try the edge experimentally on the sparse gray hairs on his forearm, return to his patient whetting. Perhaps he had a need for a blade so painstakingly sharpened, Binder thought. Perhaps he was a butcher, a brain surgeon, a midnight slasher.

He saw Corrie and Stephie cross the street and go into the beauty shop, Corrie pausing as she pushed open the door, turning to raise a hand. Birds bright as mockup birds of chrome and tinfoil foraged the withering grass, and they along with Corrie's crisp dark curls seemed untouched by the suffocating heat. The old man's longsleeved chambray shirt was dark with perspiration across the back and armpits, sweat soaked through the collar buttoned against his stark neck.

Your name wouldn't be Charlie Cagle, would it?

Well it might, if you ain't takin up money or sellin insurance.

I'm not doing either one, Binder said.

What are you doin then?

Just passing the time of day. Been hot, hasn't it?

July is like that. You from around here, young feller?

I live out at the old Beale place.

Say you do? I allowed that place was boarded up now.

No. The people who owned it kept it up. The house is in good shape.

You a married man?

Yes, Binder said, watching the rectangle of sundrenched glass that was the door to the beauty shop.

I reckon she must be a right nervy little gal then. To live out there on that place.

Why do you say that?

It's so far from town and kind of back in them woods and all. You got to admit it ain't the cheerfulest-lookin place in the world.

It's not that for sure.

That her went in that store and thowed her hand at ye a minute ago?

Yes.

I guess them old peafowls in there gives her a earful about the Beale place then, the old man said dryly. Reckon you might have to tote her to get her back home. Or hogtie her and drag her one.

We've been out there two weeks. Nothing's happened, Binder said, thinking of the dog, the watchful yellow ungleaming eyes and black flag of a tail dropping against the cornrows.

Well, I lived in this county all my life and all I ever heard was tales folks told. So-and-so seen this, heard that. Jesse Bright he was back in there digging ginseng one time. He thought he knowed where he was, keepin his directions by the sun, but then it clouded up, come up a rain and he got off in a long hollow and didn't know no mor'n a blind hog where he was. He blundered around awhile and said finally he started hearin this music, purty and far off, and just set down on a stump and took it all in.

What sort of music?

Just purty music. Said he ort to been scared but wadn't. Somebody singin, but he said it sounded so far off he couldn't make out the words. Said it sounded like a real purty church song.

You believe that?

I don't believe it or disbelieve it. I'm just tellin you is all.

When the Beale haunting first began, the spirit or whatever she was used to sing gospel songs, didn't she?

Is that a fact? Well, that was a mighty long time ago. How would you know a thing like that?

I read a book about the Beale place.

Say you did. What are you, some kind of writer?

No, Binder said, grinning. Just some kind of reader.

Writers come down here off and on. Folks puts em on somethin fierce, tells em the awfulest old bunch of bullshit you ever heard.

Cagle began to whittle from a length of red cedar, the soft, curling shavings mounding delicately in the lap of his overalls. Binder could smell the aromatic cedar. He thought inanely of the time the old man seemed to possess so much of, the almost ceremonial preparation of the knife just to whittle something ultimately unrecognizable from softened wood.

I spect a lot of that Beale haunt stuff was made up just to pass the time, don't you? Folks didn't have no television sets to hunker in front of back then. They had to addle their brains some other way.

You may be right, Binder said.

I may not be plumb right. It was a man claimed to be a writer come in here in the forties, not many years after Owen Swaw killed hisself. He was from up north somers. He prowled around out there a long time one summer huntin ghosts, then he left or I reckon he did. I never did know if he got his book wrote or not.

Did you ever meet him?

Shor I met him, the old man said, his tone insinuating that Binder had subtly insulted him. He looked me up special cause everbody figured I knowed Owen as well as anybody did. Me and Owen was cuttin timber right before he went crazy as shit and took a choppin ax to his old lady. He was a nice feller, this here writer was. Had a way of listenin like he was just soakin you up. Soft-spoken, talked with some kind of accent, said he was from Hungry or somers.

What was his name?

I was just tryin to think. Sunderson, somethin like that.

Sunderson doesn't sound Hungarian.

Somewheres over there across the waters. It don't matter. All I'm sayin is you find a feller wears them hornrimmed glasses and got a college degree in his hippocket and you listen to his talking about that ghost stuff real serious and you put a little more weight to it. He was a doctor of somethin, some kind of doctor.

Corrie came out of the beauty shop, Stephie behind her. They got into the pickup and it slowly backed onto the street, eased down and reparked before the A&P.

You got a nice little family there.

Thank you. How come Swaw killed his family?

Nobody every knowed. I reckon he just went crazy all of a sudden. Killed his wife in the toolshed and went in the house and commenced on his daughters. Got three out of four of them and then he shot himself. Or so they say.

You don't think that was the way of it?

Cagle was silent a moment. I don't know, he finally said. Somethin was botherin Owen. I drunk a beer or two with him the day he shot hisself.

What happened to the last girl?

She was put up for adoption. I imagine a thing like that happen to you when you was a kid would mess you up some.

I imagine so.

She's hollerin at you.

Binder looked up. Corrie had come out on the sidewalk, was in fact not hollering but beckoning with an arm. I got to go tote groceries, he said. I'll see you again.

You want to know what I think?

Sure I do.

That place is charmed.

It's what?

Charmed. All of it, the whole fifteen thousand acres. All of it old man Beale ever had title to.

Charmed by who? Or what?

I don't know. Do I look two hundred years old?

Well, did you ever hear or see anything out there? Funny lights, voices?

No, I never.

The old man arose and closed the knife, brushed off the front of his overalls. The soft nighweightless shavings fell plumb in the windless air, settled like shredded gossamer about his shoes. Listen, he said, somebody starts beatin on your door in the middle of the night you don't have to get up and open the door, do ye? Your telephone rings, you can let her ring can't ye? What

I'm tellin you is you let stuff like that in. Me, let's just say I heard somebody knockin. I left the door shut, though.

He saw with a kind of momentary and icecold clarity that the place had attracted them, had drawn them as a magnet draws iron filings, dangling its erotic past before already faulted vessels, biding its time during the tenancy of those it could not use, waiting.

You let such as that in.

The Old Beale Homeplace, 1933

Owen Swaw had a fight with his landlord over a broken double-shovel plow and found himself abruptly thrown off the place in midsummer, the crop he had planned to share in contention and hard feelings all around. Swaw had a wife and four daughters that ranged from grown to nearly grown.

Lawed off a place we lived on four year, the woman said, bitterly. Her name was Lorene. Lawed off and not even by a sheriff. Lawed off by a man a sheriff sent. If I'da had sons stead of daughters I'da never been throwed off to begin with. Them as can done gets em, she said. Them as don't makes do as best they can.

Swaw was used to hard times. He had known no other. He was used to field peas and cornbread when he had them and he was used to not having them too. He was used to shotgun shacks with cracks you could have thrown a good-sized housecat through and floors through whose cracks a man could watch his chickens scratching for worms, if he was lucky enough to possess any chickens. In 1933 a man on Swaw's status level was a good deal more likely to possess a housecat than he was a chicken, and Swaw was no exception.

He was used to bonechilling cold in the wintertime with everyone crowded around a tin woodstove trying their best to keep it warm and kicking through snow to cut wood that was frozen to the heart. A sharecropper didn't have time to cut his wood in the summertime. In July and August he was used to heat that wouldn't abate even at night, when you're exhausted but awake, feeling the droplets of sweat sliding across your naked ribs, wanting to cry out Great God is the place afire, listening through the thin board walls to the woods just outside your door, the whippoorwills and crickets and owls, and knowing that day was coming and another day's work but the harder you tried to sleep the more elusive it became.

He wasn't unlike the colored man in the story. A white man and a colored man went hunting together and killed a turkey and a buzzard. At the end of the day they divided up the game. Well, the white man said, it's all the same to me. You take the buzzard and I'll take the turkey or you take the turkey and I'll take the buzzard. The colored man considered this for a time. Well, he said. It shore sounds fair but seems like I wind up with the buzzard most of the time.

Swaw was used to getting the buzzard, and he was pretty sure he had it now. He was getting more of it every day, piece by scrawny piece, from his wife and four squabbling daughters.

Then luck stepped in, a commodity with which Swaw had barely a passing acquaintance. Swaw had a friend who had one of the few steady jobs in Limestone County. He was helping log the timber off the Beale place. This friend's name was Charlie Cagle and he told Swaw he could get him a few days' work cutting timber. Cagle even let them store their household plunder, such as it was, in his barn and sleep on mattresses in an empty back room of his house.

They were logging off the original homeplace and Swaw had never seen such timber. The land had never been cut over, and these were enormous beech trees of such girth you barely had room to pull a crosscut saw back and forth, trees you'd spend half a morning felling that sounded like thunder when they finally came down.

In the thirties you worked long hours, and even in the summer the sun would be sinking when they came out with the mules past the old Beale houseplace, out of the woods and across a sloping fallow field. There was a knoll above the houseplace, and this was where the old Beale graveyard was. Once they had stopped and walked among the old graves, oblong declivities in the earth, each marked by leaning old-timey stones, marble lambs at repose and stark spires and graven angels. The hill dropped off then and there were the twin chimneys rising out of the riot of sassafras and sumac bushes like chimneys flanking an invisible house, a house no longer here. The great pear trees loaded, Swaw noticed, with green pears bigger than his feet. Swaw guessed you could have kicked your way through the brush and followed the line of the foundation rocks, but he had no desire to do so. He hadn't lost a damn thing there and he'd bet there were copperheads in there big as a man's legs.

The place gave him the all-overs anyway, but he would have been hard put to explain why. There was just a curious quality about the place. He had heard the wild tales from the time he was a kid but he didn't put any stock in them, and besides, that wasn't what he dreaded anyway. For one thing, it just never seemed to be light enough to suit him there, or perhaps that was because it was usually dusk when he passed it. For another, the place reminded him somehow of a church or some other sacred spot. A place where something solemn and momentous had happened a long time ago, steeped in a kind of patient waiting for it to happen again.

But he couldn't put it into words exactly. All he knew was he didn't like going past it and if there had been another road out he would have taken it, let Charlie Cagle laugh at him all he damn pleased. So going out he wouldn't look too close. He would walk along, weary, feeling the chambray workshirt stiffening with drying salt against his back, concentrate on the sounds the mules' hooves made over the stony field and their trace chains chiming halfmusically in the twilight, and he would be glad Charlie was walking along the wagon road with him.

Then one day in late July, Charlie broke his arm and took the mules and went in early. A hackberry they were sawing split twelve or fifteen feet in the air. It kicked back, and it was a wonder they both weren't killed. They had abandoned the saw and ran like hell, Charlie's arm flopping like a broken chicken's wing as he ran, stopping only when they heard the hackberry tumbling off down a hillside. Charlie left to get his arm set and left Swaw to trim up and mark the timber they already had down.

Of course, Swaw quit as soon as Cagle was out of sight and whittled himself a sharp stick and went to digging ginseng. Swaw would work as hard as you wanted him to as long as you watched him, but if you ever looked away he'd be long gone, almost as if the photoelectric weight of your eyes triggered some delicate sensory mechanism in his brain that kept the ax or saw moving.

Ginseng grew in abundance around these beech trees and this was found money. Clear money above his dollar a day he was going to get anyway, and digging was a sight easier than swinging a chopping ax. He liked digging it anyway. He fairly flew at it, like a miser turned loose in a roomful of money and allowed to keep all he could pick up. Before long his overall pockets were bulging.

At the cry of a whippoorwill he leapt up, startled. All at once he looked up, as if he had been awakened from sleep or in a trance. Oh shit, he said. He swallowed hard. All there was of the sun was a thin rind of gold drowning in mottled red, and a thick blue darkness was seeping out of the hollows like rising waters. A fine thread of fear ran through him. He trudged out of the woods, into the field, his gait gradually increasing until his legs were fairly scissoring across the field.

He told himself he wasn't going to look when he passed the graveyard. If you don't look, it won't be so, he told himself. He looked anyway and there was a girl sitting on Jacob Beale's tombstone, plaiting her long blond hair. She was watching Swaw with bold eyes out of a pretty, sullen face, and when she arose the pale fall of her hair swung behind her. She beckoned him.

He ran, listening to the sob of his breathing, thinking desperately that that must have been old Clyde Simpson's daughter and knowing full well all the time that Simpson's daughter was dumpy and heavyset and had a flat, stupid-looking face.

Cagle could work the mules snaking timber one-armed, so he was back to work in a few days. Swaw didn't see the girl for over a week. He kept his mouth shut, too. Then one Monday at dusk she came walking out from beneath the pear tree, humming to herself. Swaw could hear her, could hear the melody that had a haunting childhood familiarity about it, and he was about to say, There by God, now what do you say to this, when he saw Charlie's bland, preoccupied face, jaws patiently worrying their quid of tobacco. His eyes widened and he turned to the stolid mules, walking stumblefooted down the slope, stopping momentarily to crop grass, coming on when the slack pulled out of the lines, and Swaw thought, They don't see it. Nary one of them does. This is supposed to be just for me. A moment of blinding insight crept over him.

The girl was visible from the knees up, her calves and feet lost in the weeds, and even as he watched she changed from a pale sepia transparency to flesh and blood, a live woman of seventeen or eighteen standing there petulant and curiously erotic, so that he felt a rush of desire, a quickening of the blood in his groin that sickened him. She tossed her hair back. She seemed to be waiting for something. Her face was bright and conspiratorial, as if she and Swaw shared some secret the world didn't even suspect. She raised a hand and pointed at him. Her mouth opened. He could see the clean line of her teeth. Her lips moved. You, the lips mouthed.

Cagle asked, Hey, what the hell's the matter with you?

She vanished.

What?

What the hell's the matter with you?

I thought for a minute I seen something.

You look like you know damn well you did.

Did you not see anything back there?

All I see is night comin and you wastin time.

They commenced walking. Swaw didn't say anything. He began to roll a cigarette. His fingers started to shake, the little brown flakes of tobacco sifting about his moving feet, the plain rice paper shredding so that he wadded it in his fingers and dropped it covertly beside the pack.

Owen, I ain't sayin you seen somethin and I ain't sayin you didn't, but I know what I'd do if I did. I'd put it out of my mind damn quick. I'd tell myself somethin likely it could have been and I'd hold on to that as hard as I could.

Swaw didn't put it out of his mind. His mind was playing with her image like a cat worrying a mouse. She went just like that, like blowin out a coal-oil lamp. He wondered where she went to. He thought she went somewhere he remembered with a vague familiarity, someplace he had been years ago.

More luck. Good for some, not so good for others. Clyde Simpson had been sharecropping Beale's land. He had the crop laid by and was waiting for fall, enjoying the pause before harvest time. In the white still heat of noonday he ran a snarling black dog out of his cornfield. It kept snapping at the cuffs of his overalls, and when he bent over to pick up a clod of dirt to throw at it his heart burst and he died there with the hot sun in his eyes and the Mastiff watching him from the edge of the cornfield.

Beale was in a quandary. Here he had a fine corn crop already making and no one to tend it and gather it come autumn, save Simpson's widow and his simpleminded daughter.

A man named Hinson told it at the Snow White Café: he was wonderin who he could get. Hell, everybody that was worth a damn already had a crop goin. He's too tight to hire it gathered. Swaw's name came up somehow and somebody said, You don't want Swaw. That tore it. You know how contrary the old son of a bitch is. He studied about it. I want Swaw, he said. Swaw's the very feller I need. Swaw don't know how lucky he is.

I wouldn't mind workin that land, a man named Qualls said. But I wouldn't want a man to have a stroke and die just so I'd get it. That ain't the kind of luck I want.

Beale sent word for Swaw to come in and talk to him. He didn't live on the Beale land. He lived in a tall redbrick house on Walnut Street in town and he didn't lower himself to drive out to Cagle's and see Swaw there. He figured he could work a better deal in his imposing study. He offered Swaw a tenant's share of the ungathered crop: half the crop to Beale, twenty-five percent to the Widow Simpson, twenty-five percent to Swaw.

Swaw said he'd think about it.

Beale couldn't believe his ears. He had offered Swaw a tenancy on the finest farm in the county and the occupancy of a house any other dirt farmer in the county would have mortgaged his soul for, and Swaw said he'd think about it. At that moment, though he didn't know it, Swaw's fate was sealed. Beale was determined to have him now.

What do you mean you'll study on it? Lorene asked him. Us with no roof of our own over our head and Mama's bed settin out there in a mule barn. It don't seem to me you got anything to study on.

That place gives me the all-overs, Swaw said sullenly.

Look around you. Looks like seein your daughters livin piled up in the same old room like hogs would give you the all-overs, she said.

The analogy had never occurred to Swaw before, but he did note that, strewn out across the floor of the little moonlit room, their bulky bodies did remind him of sleeping hogs, and during the day they'd be just as useless, couched somewhere in the shade grunting to each other, probably, he thought, about some boar: all they seemed to think about anymore was men and just showin up for feeding time, he thought. Fightin over what's in the trough.

And about as shameless as hogs, too. He couldn't walk around the corner of the house without catching one squatting to pee. It had got to where they didn't even leap up anywhere adjusting their skirts. They'd just sit there with their bare cheeks shining moonlike and gaze at him stolidly as grazing cows. Or hogs. They'd set across from him or he guessed any man who happened to be there with their skirts hiked up and their legs spraddled out, gleaming like barked-up whiteoak logs.

All except Retha.

Retha was the youngest, and she might have been a changeling the little people left, she was so different. She was so different in fact that Swaw had always felt some vague unspoken unease about her parentage. Perhaps she wasn't his. He'd almost rather believe she was the only one who was.

Lorene was big and rawboned and she had hands and arms like a man's. Her voice was masculine, too, a coarse sandpapery whiskey voice, though she didn't even drink. And all the daughters except Retha seemed to be growing up divested of any mannerisms Swaw had been raised to consider feminine, save the essential and quixotic fact of their sex itself, the moonoriented flowing of their menses.

Lorene and the four daughters had already felt a subtle shifting of their social standing. They had been offered the Beale place. They wouldn't own a scrap of land, but they would have a strong house and what was left of the Simpson crop. They were still oneeyed, but they were, after all, in the kingdom of the blind. They went to look at the Beale house, touring it with a proprietary air before the Widow Simpson had even begun to think of packing her bags. They came back for three consecutive days, and on the third they saw Widow Simpson's brothers loading her furniture into two wagons. The Swaws sat on the wagon seat watching from a stand of cypress like distant spectators at a funeral. The horses stirred and the wagons began to roll soundlessly. The mirror of a tilting chifferobe winked at them in the sun like a heliograph.

Swaw was not far behind in the awareness of his altered level at the bottom of society's sediment. A man long accustomed to walking anywhere he had to go, he suddenly had a fine team of horses at his disposal. There was a rubbertired wagon, not yet two seasons old and with the red paint not even weathered off, that was a source of great wonder to Swaw. It was the closest thing to an automobile he'd ever ridden in.

Swaw is a fool about that rubbertired wagon, they said about him in the Snow White Café. He don't never walk no more. Thinks he's too good. I bet Swaw won't go down to the shithouse lessen he hooks up that rubbertired wagon.

Swaw piddled about the place waiting for the corn to mature and for frost and he spent much of the time before the dead fireplace with his feet propped up, slowly turning the pages of the new fall and winter Sears Roebuck catalog. He was making lists in his head of all the things his twenty-five percent of Simpson's crop would buy. And he wasn't the only one making lists. A veritable epidemic of list-making ensued.

Swaw was already thinking of next year's crop. There was a turtleback Hudson Hornet setting in the second row of Toot Grimes' car lot that made him want an automobile so bad there was something achingly erotic about it. He hungered for the feel of the steering wheel in his hands so deeply that he dreamed about it at night. He imagined driving it down the main street of Beales Gap, his head reared back a little, his eyes looking neither to the right nor to the left. He might even start going to church. Church would be a good place to show off his automobile. He saw himself on the way out, his dark suit crisp with newness, his boiled white shirt blinding in the sun, his black hair slicked down and gleaming pomade. Women turning to look at him speculatively.

All this was before the rats began in the walls. They began first in the girls' room. He didn't hear about it for a few days.

What rats? he asked. Rats doin what?

Eatin, they said. Chewin in the walls. Grindin their old teeth together.

Long as they ain't chewin you, just pay em no mind, he said.

A shriek in the night brought him barefoot down the moonlit hall. The oldest girl was cowering in the corner of the room, half naked, white as a bedsheet. There was a rat in the bed with me, the girl said, shuddering. I could feel it rubbing against my leg.

You get some goddamn clothes on or I'll be rubbing something against that hind end, Swaw said.

He went through the bedclothes a piece at a time until there was a white mound in the center of the floor. Nothing. With the coal-oil lamp in his hand and his shadow humped and broken against the wall he searched for holes in the baseboard, in the paneling, for anywhere a rat could have gone.

It ain't nowhere a rat could have went, he said. If it ain't nowhere it could have gone and it ain't no rat in here, then you ain't seen no rat.

I know a rat when I see one, the girl said, and I seen that one jump off the bed. I heard it hit the floor.

Get in that bed and get to sleep, Swaw said. I got work to do in the morning, and I'm damn tired of hearin about rats.

When he was back in bed they began in earnest: a rising ocean of rat sounds, as if a veritable legion of them were steadfastly gnawing the structure into sawdust that would ultimately come sifting over their heads as they lay abed. The sounds spread incrementally, infinitesimally as air, over the floorboards to the footboards of the bed itself and ascending on the wooden bed, steady and unrelenting, gnawing over all the bed at once. He lay clutching the covers.

Lorene awoke, drowsily listening until the sounds brought her wide awake and apprehensive.

What on earth?

It sounds like rats, he said, unnecessarily.

She didn't answer. The noise rose in volume as if controlled
by some vituperative force. A faint and far-off squeaking of the
young so that Swaw saw in his mind great hordes of soft pink rats
clutching their mothers, the elder rats gray and malign, tails like
rattail files. Lord God, she said.

It ain't no rats, Swaw said. You can smell a goddamn gopher
rat and there ain't no smell at all in this house.

The words were no sooner said than a stench of rats saturated
the room, unspeakably fetid and overpowering, instantaneous,
foul and malefic, just abruptly *there*, the house stifling with it. Swaw
lent gagging over the side of the bed, struggled up.

They ran out choking and retching into the night. The six
of them silently aligned before the dark house. It set still and
impassive as if it were watching them back.

Swaw cleared his throat and spat. He had the taste of rats in
the back of his mouth.

What we need us is a good housecat, the woman said.

Swaw just looked at her. He didn't say a word.

He was abroad early the next morning. The rubbertired wagon
stood before Judge Beale's house. Swaw sat across from Beale in
the oak-paneled study. Beale trimmed his nails with a nail clipper.
Swaw talked of rats and watched Beale's disbelieving face and
listened to the nail clippers make little snick-snicks of punctuation.

Swaw spoke of rats at some length. When he had finished
Beale just shook his head. There were no rats, Beale said. The
house had been fumigated in the spring for bugs and poison and
traps set for rats. Besides, there had never been a problem with
rats. The place had always been scrupulously kept. Swaw said
there was for goddamn sure a problem with rats now, and if
Beale thought he was a liar he could drive out there tonight and
see for himself. The judge declined. He gave Swaw an enigmatic

smile and a chit for the grocery store good for twenty pounds of rat poison.

Swaw came out angry and sweating. He balled the chit up and threw it in a hedgerow bordering Beale's lawn. He knew in his heart there was no need in hauling in a sack of rat poison.

He was right, too. They never heard them again. The house was bored with rats.

The summer drew on, warm and mellow. In the soft, moist nights the bottomland alongside Sinking Creek was beset with fireflies, great phosphorescent droves of them drifting like St. Elmo's fire through the cool blue dusk.

In the fields the ears of corn lengthened and hardened, the leaves yellowed and withered, then grew brittle. The fields that bordered them turned bright yellow with goldenrod; wild apricots ripened on their dying vines strung on fences, withered globes of dusty gold, and the air was heavy with their musky perfume.

They were briefly happy.

Random as the fireflies, his three eldest daughters were coming and going at all hours of the day and night, as if they had all come into heat simultaneously and word of it sent abroad into the land so that in early September Swaw found himself beleaguered every night by swain from all up and down Sinking Creek, old rustyankled country boys with red necks and hardons and old highbacked rolling junkers held together by spit and baling wire and blind luck, weighting the harvest dusks with the smell of oil burning engines, the stench of rubber from smoking tires. Drunken laughter echoed in the still dark, his daughters with it, raucous and meaningless as calling crows or harpies.

I never seen the goddamn like in my life, he raged to Lorene. Lately he was mostly in a rage. He was sleeping badly.

Lorene just seemed pleased they had entered into an active social life. Let em have their fun, she told him, adding darkly, I never had any. You seen to that.

I aim to put a stop to it, he said.

They just poplar, Lorene said.

Popular was not quite the concept Swaw was struggling with. He would hear them leaving in the old highbacked sedans, gone a while, back once more. Then after a while horns blowing, wild mindless laughter, gone again. He wished for sons. At least sons would be at somebody else's house worrying the hell out of them.

At first they sat on the stone doorsteps and plied him with splo whiskey, spoke with transparent craft of the weather, crops, the likelihood of an early winter. Biding their time until they could be gone in a cloud of oily blue smoke and a roar of rusted mufflers, gone to the beer joints at Flatwoods, the show, the woods. They grew emboldened. At last they just drove up and honked their horns. They quit bringing him whiskey, too.

He found a used condom down by the creek. It lay drying in the morning sun, like some arcane form of life beached here by distant seas. He took it up on the end of a stick and threw it in the creek, cursing all the while. They poplar, all right, he said to himself. Pussy was always purty well thought of in these parts.

He commenced running them off. He'd run out into the yard shouting, waving his double-barreled shotgun, maybe fire off a round or two just to hear the shot rattle in the trees. You'd hear Model Ts cranking all the way to Shipps Bend. But they were getting bolder, like wild dogs held at bay by a circle of light. While he was nailing up the front door they were kicking down the back, and there were nights he ran off the same bunch three or four times.

One night a soft mewing noise drew him behind the toolshed. Bowered by honeysuckle, he came upon a naked couple stricken by moonlight, laboring away. The sons of bitches were even bringing their own blankets now. They didn't hear him until he was upon them. He could smell the raw aroused smell of them, could feel his own member thicken. He raised a booted foot and slammed into the boy's naked nates. The boy went squalling like a ribkicked dog, hauling at his breeches as he went, whirling where the dark opened up and leering back at Swaw.

Swaw didn't have his gun, and he couldn't find a rock.

He couldn't keep them in the fields either. He'd harness both teams, take one wagon and head for the lower bottoms after getting them started in the upper, but he'd be no more than out of sight when some old boy would saunter out of the brush with a shit-eating grin on his face and they'd be long gone. He was trying to get a crop in, and he'd come in at midday to eat and they'd be lounging around the porch. You had to kick one aside to find a place to sit down.

Piss on it, he said to himself. I wash my hands of em. They can root like hogs or die. He felt sure things were becoming unmanageable. He felt how surely the center was not holding, how adroitly things fell apart. He felt like a man trying to stuff a pumped-up inner tube into a shoebox. He'd stomp one side in and the other would pop up. He'd hold both ends and the middle would leap out like a jack-in-the-box until the shoebox was demolished, the inner tube still just as round and fat and uncontained as ever.

Swaw came down the slope with a rolled towsack under his arm. He carried a hoe to part the weeds with. He moved carefully toward the pear tree, studying the ground beneath his feet as he walked. The air was winy with the smell of ripe pears.

When he was sure there were no snakes about he moved with more confidence. He began to pick pears from the lower branches and stuff them into the sack. He worked hurriedly. The pears were warm to his touch and seemed to have stored all the fugitive warmth of summer beneath their yellowbrown skin. The ground beneath the tree was strewn with fermenting pears, and all around him was a steady drone of insects.

Sitting on a mosscovered stone he ate a pear, slicing it off a section at a time with his pocket knife, slapping away onehanded the yellow jackets the juice attracted. He was staring off below the homeplace, where the earth curved gently into a hollow, when for no reason at all he thought: something is going to happen.

The wry air seemed to alter, to thicken. His vision of the world darkened as if the sun reached the glade filtered by an eerie shadow. He could hear a child's voice singing. A child in a green dress swung from a grapevine, blond hair strung out behind her. It felt to Swaw as if the skin of his body was tightening. He watched the sunburnt hairs on his forearms stand erect, the flesh beneath them crinkle with gooseflesh. There was a popping sound in his eardrum, or a dull far-off roaring like water. His mouth was dry.

Humming to herself, the girl came out of the brush into what had once been the yard. She seemed not to notice Swaw. She had moved so swiftly that his breath caught in his throat. There was no discernible motion of feet or of legs, but rather a smooth movement as if she were gliding. He could see the tree branches and brush behind her. She ascended to the level of the rubblestrewn foundation, as if unaware that there was no longer a floor there.

Swaw felt drained of volition, lethargic, frozen to the stone where he sat. The girl was watching him. He saw that she was not a child, but a young woman, the flaxenhaired girl he'd seen before. She watched Swaw with cold cat's eyes. Her fingers were slowly unbuttoning the top of her long dress. She slipped it down about her hips, stood bare to the waist, her hands cupping her breasts, which were very white in the sun. Her nipples seemed the texture and color of pale pink rosebuds. Her face was innocent and childlike but her eyes seemed to be taunting him. Her hands caught under her sharp breasts, upthrust them, as if she were mocking him with them. He was on his feet and stumbling toward her before he realized it.

She was gone. He heard soft, derisive laughter behind him. A thrown pear struck the foundation stones at his feet. He stood looking at it. It had split against the rocks, and hornets worked the ripe flesh, buzzing a onenote drone of gluttony.

For two weeks she had been coming to him while he slept. In the dream, if it was a dream, it seemed to be autumn, the time of year after the first frost. The trees were baring and the grass felt sere beneath his feet and the white road lay dusted with moonlight. Once a falling leaf touched his face, a golden sepia cast like an aged photograph.

He felt strange to himself, and he had no words to explain it. He felt bigger and curiously older, slowmoving. His mouth hurt. The countryside looked subtly different too. There in the moonlight, the trees seemed lower and closer together. The wind in their branches was foreign to him, whispered of bitter winters he'd never known.

The toolshed reared starkly against the heavens. The door swung soundlessly on oiled hinges. Inside the air was thick with the smell of new pine boards. He'd come across the floorboards pulling off his clothes.

She would be on a pallet of quilts against the wall and at his arrival she would rise to her knees on the quilts and shuck the dress off over her head. She wore nothing beneath it. She'd raise her hands to smooth her hair, the moonlight through the cracks rendering her body all black and silver, silver face and throat and sharp, pointed breasts, the darker pubic triangle under her silver belly. Something mysterious and profound, the very negation of her flesh.

He would fall with her onto the pallet, her hips already arching to meet him.

From the night Swaw had the first dream the house was quiet. Satisfied, perhaps. There were no rats, no lights bobbing toward the barn, no singing. No one save Swaw saw or heard anything you would not expect to see or hear.

Except for one occasion Swaw never heard about: Retha was hulling out walnuts in the hollow above the barn, and for some reason she looked up. Below her a man was walking toward the hall of the barn. He was an old man with muttonchop whiskers and he walked with his left leg dragging. He strode into the hall of the barn and out of her line of vision. She kept waiting for him to walk out the other side but he never did. She never mentioned it to anyone. He had looked so like a flesh-and-blood man it was some time before it occurred to her he could have been anything else, and by then it was too late.

What's the matter with you? she asked him.

Nothin in this round world, Swaw said.

Then why are you in bed ever night before good dark? How come you ain't never got a word to say to nobody?

Swaw pulled the covers over his chest. Through the window he watched the grove of cypress across the creek slowly vanish in sweet darkness.

Hell, I'm tired, he said. I been tryin to gather a corn crop singlehanded. I don't see nobody offerin to help, neither.

I do what I can, she said. I been in the field same as you.

I know it. I meant them worthless girls.

You too tired to talk awhile? I get lonesome with them out courtin ever night, and Retha ain't never had nothin much to say for herself. She sat on the edge of the bed.

I seen you prowlin around that old toolshed. You got a bottle hid in there.

Swaw had closed his eyes. He didn't say anything. She sat there for a time in silence and then after a while he heard her sigh and then the corresponding sigh of the bedsprings when she got up. The door closed behind her.

Swaw opened his eyes. He lay waiting for the girl.

The rains of early fall began. The sky went slategray, dripped with leaden weeping. Forlorn and lostlooking birds foraged the barren fields.

He saw the sign first. Whoa, he called. The team ceased, the wagon halted, he began to hear the rain soft in the trees. He spelled out the words on the sign, his lips moving slowly as he did so. A TEMPLE OF THE HOLY JESUS REVIVAL, the first line read. In smaller print, the second: NIGHTLY AT 7:00.

Git up, he called. He snapped the lines. Around the curve he saw the tent and the old car. He saw them simultaneously, the old olivedrab tent set up in the field, ropes running taut to stakes driven at an angle in the earth, the hearselooking old sedan parked before it in the mud.

We'll see about this, Swaw said. He stopped the team again, this time pulling them to the side of the road. He climbed down, checked to see if the groceries were covered with the tarpaulin. He took a halfpint bottle from the back pocket of his overalls and canted to the light. It was almost empty. He drained the bottle and tossed it into the ditch and climbed the embankment to the field, rain sitting on the brim of the old felt hat he wore.

The field was a sucking quagmire of mud. Gray water shoaled in wide, shallow pools. Swaw picked his way between them toward the wagon. He saw no one about the tent but he could see a man's profile through the glass. Were it Swaw, he would have been trying to get the car back onto the solid surface of the road, but the man behind the steering wheel was just serenely watching it rain.

The car had once been black but the weather had faded it to sort of lusterless gray, the exact texture and color of old tar. The glass was cranked down to show a young man with red hair, bright as a rooster's comb and shiny with Brilliantine. The man had gray eyes and acne-pitted skin.

How do, brother, he said. He thrust a freckled hand into the rain. Swaw took the hand and gave it a perfunctory pump and then dropped it.

Do you know where you're at? he asked.

Yes, I do, the man said complacently. I'm settin in a fine automobile watchin God's own rain fall.

You in the middle of Joseph Beale's pasture is where you are, Swaw said. And he don't 'low no trespassin.

The man nodded. He smiled, keeping his lips compressed, as if he had bad teeth. A fey dimple appeared in each cherubic cheek. Arrangements have been made with Mr. Beale, he said.

You must of arranged to be here awhile. I was you, I'd a been tryin to get out of here.

It's God Almighty's rain, friend. He's not worryin about it.

God Almighty hisself couldn't drive a T-Model Ford through mud half kneedeep.

God's love can splinter you to the heart like lightning killin a tree. Don't blaspheme, brother. Have you been baptized?

Not in some time, Swaw said.

If you're baptized in the blood, once is all it takes.

I've backslid a time or two.

The preacher was watching him with level eyes.

You ain't going to get no meetin here tonight anyway.

Two is a meetin, friend, if one of em is in need of salvation
and the othern is equipped to provide it. Don't the Bible say
wheresoever two or more are meet in My name, there I shall be
also?

I reckon it does.

You ever handled the serpents?

Ever what?

Handled poisonous serpents when the spirit of God was on
ye? Drank strychnine and lived to tell it?

Lord no. And don't plan to.

Ever held your head in the fire and nary a hair was singed?

No.

Then you ain't baptized and never have been. You ain't
never had the gift. The gift of salvation, neighbor. The faith to
know that you can handle poison and serpents and God's love is
between your face and the fangs. That you can drink strychnine
and know your stomach is coated with a salvation that poison can't
eat through. That's the gift. Any of you ain't true baptized, your
soul will twist and turn in Hell like a paper burnin in the fireplace.

Jesus Christ never handled no snake, Swaw said. Never drunk
no strychnine, neither.

Jesus died so the likes of me and you could stand here in
the rain and argue about it, friend. That's the price he paid for
salvation. Me and you could get it a little cheaper.

Where you got these snakes?

Got em in boxes right inside that tent yonder. Got em in cages.

I figured bein as they didn't hurt you you'd just let em run loose like a housedog.

The preacher looked at him with a pitying contempt. The spirit ain't always on ye, neighbor. It comes and goes like the season.

What kind you got?

Copperheads. Timber rattlers. Got a cottonmouth big as your arm. A little coral snake I got in Texas pretty as a silk handkerchief.

Let's see em.

Why, sure.

The preacher got out into the rain. He rolled the glass up and closed the car door. He had on shiny lowquarters and he picked his way between the mudholes. They moved toward the tent, drummed down by the rain. The preacher pulled aside a flap door and Swaw followed him in. It was darker inside, and for a moment he could see only the white shirt of the preacher. He was conscious of the smell of new pine lumber, as if he had been in the toolshed of his dream. Then he saw the flat boxes along one wall. They were of pine shelving, and they had holes augured into the sides. For ventilation, Swaw guessed.

My little sister, she tends em, the preacher was saying. He had approached the stacked boxes. She's got a gift with serpents. Don't think no more of pickin em up than you would playin with a puppy. They love her, too. They know she takes care of em.

He casually opened the lid of one of the boxes as he spoke. The lid was hinged and it swung open smoothly. Swaw involuntarily stepped back, then saw the snake in the box was restrained by an inner lid of locking and by a layer of wire mesh. It was a copperhead coiled on a bed of straw, motionless, bright head aloft as if it were listening to some far-off sound Swaw had not heard as yet.

That's my little sister yonder, the preacher said, pointing, and Swaw turned, so caught up in the snake that he was aware of the girl's presence for the first time. She stood in the corner facing an isinglass window of the tent watching him and slowly turned. Swaw suddenly felt chilled, aware of the cold layers of wet clothing against his skin, and for a dizzy second he thought he was going to faint, for the world darkened and everything looked vague and far away. The preacher was still talking, but sounds had diminished and Swaw couldn't understand him.

Swaw had known her the instant she began to turn, had in some dark cobwebbed corner of his mind known her surely before that by the long flaxen hair and the shape of her body beneath the dress. She was watching him with eyes luminous and compassionless as a cat's. It was the girl who had beckoned him from Jacob Beale's tombstone.

Dark fell early. The rain had ceased. They came up the old roadbed by lanternlight, the bevy of giggling girls leading the way. When they reached the field there was no light in it, no sign of voices.

I don't see nothin, the woman said. There was accusation in her voice. I never heard nothin about no camp meetin neither.

It was right about here, Swaw said. He seemed to be speaking to himself. He raised the lantern, and by the yellow light his sallow face looked carved from dark burnished wood. He peered into the darkness. A chorus of frogs called from the wet field.

You come in drunkern a bicycle, she taunted. Likely you dreamed it or just made it up for meanness.

He crossed the ditch. Below him he could hear water running in it. He went up the embankment and over the splitrail fence. He could feel morning glory vines and sawbriars tugging at him as he crossed into the field. The water was shoemouth deep and rose about his feet. The water looked opaque and illusory, the depth thrown into question, and for a moment there was something sinister about the barren field.

What are you lookin for?

He swung the lantern in an arc. There was something of desperation in his choppy movements. Dry weeds, the unbroken earth in the bare spots stood out in stark relief. Tire tracks, he said. And again, Tire tracks, goddamn it.

Tire tracks, she said contemptuously.

The girls had fallen into a sullen silence. There was to be no meeting, no gaiety, no singing, no snakes. No salvation.

Boat tracks more likely, the eldest said, a harpy's echo of her mother.

Swaw didn't reply. He hunkered to the wet earth. With his hand he parted the tall grass, saw only the rainwashed black loam. Hunkered there in the darkness, he felt before himself a door, madness already raising the hand to knock.

Madness sniffing at his tracks like an unwanted dog. Madness would escort him the rest of the way there, clutching at him and whispering adulterous secrets in his ear.

He could see them through the sundrenched window picking the last of the fieldpeas. Lorene and the three eldest, a gaggle of bonneted women moving through the garden above the creek, picking the dry peas into their aprons, transferring them to burlap bags. Hogs in the field, he thought. Beyond them the silver water metallic in the sun.

The house seemed locked in silence so intense he felt he could hear it. A buzzing undercurrent like electricity, the air harsh and surreal. He was waiting, but he didn't know for what.

Daddy? Retha called. Her voice was muffled through the walls.

His hand released the sheer curtain. What? he said. He could still see them, spectral and distant, through the gauzy cloth.

Come in here a minute.

He went into the hall and to the bedroom door. He opened it.
Good God, girl, he said. He could hardly speak. The sight of her made
his breath catch in his throat. She was standing naked in a foottub, her
body lathered with soapsuds. She had washed her hair and it clung
wetly to her head, hung in curly tendrils that halfobstructed her soapy
breasts, small and perfectly formed. His eyes fell to the smooth white
of her belly, the dark patch of pubic hair white with lather. The long
white expanse of her legs hurt his chest.

Will you git me a towel off the clothesline?

He forced himself to back through the door. He slammed it to
behind him. He could hear her voice through the door, querulous,
a childlike whine crept into it.

What's the matter, Daddy?

He could hear their voices nearing the house, the girls snig-
gering about something. The old woman's coarse monotone
cutting through. He could see the harsh sun white through the
screen. They ascended the steps into his sunlit vision.

Daddy, she called again.

He returned with the towel and handed it through, extending
his arm without fully opening the door.

Later that day Swaw opened the door to the toolshed, had already
reached for the bottle he had hid above the door lintel. Half the
floor had been wrecked out before Swaw's time, and he found
Retha sitting on the edge of the floor watching him. He turned,
startled, then began to search all around as if he had come in for
some particular tool.

What are you lookin for?

Never you mind what I'm lookin for, Retha. What are you
doin in here?

Just sittin in here where it's quiet.

Go on and get out of there. You're liable to get copperhead bit.

She got up reluctantly. I like it in here, she said.

Why? It seems a funny place to come and sit.

I don't know.

Swaw liked it out here and he didn't know why either. All he knew was that the door of the toolshed seemed to close off the rest of the world. When you were in the toolshed things you worried about didn't bother you. Everything was timeless in here. There was a different perspective to things. In fact, there weren't any things, as if the toolshed and its handhewn cedar door was the sum totality of existence, finite, the only thing there was. Swaw didn't want to share it.

Go help your mama get in the last of them tomaters, he said, and don't let me catch you back in here again. You git snakebit you'd die fore I could git you to a doctor, even with that wagon and team.

When she was gone he got down the bottle and drank, then sat on the wooden floorboards, feeling the warm assurance of alcohol feeding all through him. He rolled himself a Country Gentleman smoke and lit it, watched the blue smoke shift hazily in the columns of spilled light.

He heard laughter. A girl's laughter, children, secretive and faint, and for some reason he suddenly felt like a trespasser or eavesdropper. He knew subconsciously he was listening to something that had not been said for his ears.

Yet consciously he thought, Them damn trifling girls. He thought about getting up to go look and he was just about to do so when a feminine voice no more than eight or ten inches from his ear said quite distinctly, Don't do that no more, Daddy.

Swaw was up like a shot. Damn you, Retha, he said. He looked wildly about. No one, nothing save bits of straw drifting in moted light. He threw open the door and flooded the shed with hot sunlight. Retha was going through the garden gate, a basket swinging in her hand. He heard the hinges creak as the door closed behind her.

Saturday morning he went to a movie. He sat in the darkness and watched the flickering screen. He couldn't concentrate on the film. It was all horses and gunfire, stagecoaches and buckboards running away. A blondhaired girl was beset with troubles the buckskin hero must set to rights. He wished desperately his life had the stark simplicity of a movie. Black was immediately distinguishable from white, right from wrong.

He felt beleaguered on all sides. The old woman and his daughters were mad at him. She was afraid they were going to be run off the Beale place. Beale was looking for him, mad about the corn still standing in the field, he guessed.

He was vaguely aware of the voices of children around him in the darkness. He could feel the halfpint bottle through his bib pocket. It was warm and comforting, a trusted familiar, a docile pet that always knew him well and showed it. He took it out and unscrewed the cap and drank. It was bad whiskey, an evil smell uncoiling in the darkness, and his stomach almost revolted. He felt hot vomit rise in his throat. He swallowed and closed his throat and suppressed it. After a minute he felt a little better. Every small victory counted now.

Hey, they don't allow no drinkin in here, an old woman said behind him.

Swaw turned around. He could barely make her out. A bitter, dried-up old woman, the very embodiment of reprimand. Shut up, you old whore, he said. He didn't bother to lower his voice. He could hear the sharp intake of the woman's breath.

The theatre fell abruptly silent about him. Swaw went back to watching the movie.

Sepia sagebrush images flickered there. A Never Never Land that never was. Black villains, heroes and heroines pure as the driven snow. Injustice settled with a gloved fist, a .45 revolver that seemed to never need reloading. Might makes right.

He felt the whiskey soaking through a tide of warm flames flickering in his flesh. The movie seemed to be ending. The heroine embraced the hero. Her lithe arms encircled his neck. Mash them titties agin him, Swaw thought. Past his broad shoulder she looked directly at Swaw. Her hair was long and blond, wavering to her shoulders and ending in a mass of curls. Her eyes were calculating as a cat's. Her lips parted, and he could see the white predatory line of her teeth. Her lips moved. *You*, she said above the romantic swell of music. He lurched to his feet.

Hey, sit down there, a voice called.

He didn't turn. He stood looking at the screen. A catcall of voices arose, a Coke cup wadded around a core of ice caught him hard in the temple. He half fell, caught on the row of seats in front of him, whirled peering into the darkness. Who done that? he cried. Which one of you little cocksuckers thowed that at me?

Lord God, the old woman said. She struggled to her feet.

He could hear giggling beyond the circle of dark. He shambled blindly toward it, felt the ungiving wood seats hard against his shins. He leant over the row of seats, slapping at the children, swaying like a drunken bear. Son of a bitches, he told them. Little rich bastards. Another drink cup caught him between the shoulder blades and he lurched toward a new set of tormenters. After a moment he trudged up the aisle over a carpet of paper and spilt popcorn.

He wandered out blinking against the bright daylight. He sat on the curb a moment examining his barked shins. He rolled himself a smoke and lit it. He felt the bottle against his breast, cooler now, remote, alien. He knew without taking it out that it was empty. He got up and started down the street, an air of purposeful resolution about him.

In the Snow White Café he ran up with Charlie Cagle. Your old woman's a huntin ye, Cagle told him. I seen her peepin in the winder a while ago. She had a mean look on her face and a stick in her hands about this long.

Cagle was joking but Swaw wasn't in a joking mood. He sat down at the bar and ordered a draft beer. When it came he sat staring morosely into it. The hell with her, he said after a time.

Hell, I was just joshin you, Owen. I ain't even seen her.

Cagle thought Swaw looked bad. He moved as if he were in a trance. He hadn't shaved in a week or two, and from the smell of him he hadn't had a bath either. His clothes were stiff with grease and sweat; Cagle figured if Swaw climbed out of them they'd stand alone. His eyes were blackrimmed and red, as if an obscure rage flared behind them. Swaw looked like the middle of a long drunk with no end as yet in sight.

Cagle tried to draw him into conversation. How you farin out the Beale place?

All right.

You ain't seen or heard nothin out of the way?

Swaw was silent a moment. No, he said at length.

So he has, Cagle said to himself. He has, and he don't want to talk about it. But that's all right. He don't owe me nothin. I never done nothin for him only take them in when there was nowhere else to go and got a job when nobody else would hire him. I reckon that rubbertired wagon rolled him someplace where he don't remember none of that.

Pigs, Swaw said, or that's what Cagle understood him to say.

What?

All they are is goddamned hogs, gruntin and squealin. Wantin one thing and then another. He drained the mug of beer, set it down hard, and ordered another. He was going through his pockets one by one. Ultimately he dredged up two greasy ones and a handful of silver. Gimme a pack of them rubbers, he said. The barman laid the coinshaped foil package on the counter and picked up Swaw's quarter.

Hot time in the old town tonight, Owen?

What?

Nothin, the barkeep said. I was just foolin with ye.

Don't fool with me today, Swaw said.

The barkeep went to fool with somebody else.

A man two stools down had turned to study Swaw. Owen better hope that team knows the way home, he said.

Swaw didn't reply. He drained his beer, laid the change on the bar, and arose. He turned toward the door.

Where you off to, Owen?

Swaw didn't reply. He was looking directly at Cagle, but Cagle didn't think he saw him. His eyes were inwardlooking, opaque as glass buttons. He turned and went out.

When he came from putting the horses in the barn, she was standing on the doorstep blocking his way. I want to talk to you, she said.

Talk away, Swaw said.

Old man Beale was out here.

Say he was. What did he want?

What do you think he wanted? He wanted to know when you was goin to gather the rest of that corn. And I wouldn't mind knowin myself. Well?

Well, what?

When are you?

When are I, when are I, he mimicked her. When they start shipping snowballs out of hell by the boxcar load. That's when.

You drunk bastard.

He waved a disparaging hand at her and turned away.

Owen Swaw, don't you walk off and me talkin to you, she called after him.

He was walking toward the grove of liveoaks, listing a little to the left. Dusk was gathering. The western sky looked muddy red.

He came unsteadily up the slope toward the homeplace, his feet dragging a little in the high grass. Atop its summit was a yellow poplar the spring winds had blown over. He had been thinking about sawing it to lengths for wood, but he saw now his mind wasn't working right. He had brought neither ax nor saw.

The girl was sitting on the butt of the poplar log. She seemed to have been awaiting him. She had one bare foot on the ground and the other cocked on the log, her knee drawn up against her breasts. Her arms encircled the leg and her chin rested atop it. She watched him moodily from beneath her tangled blond curls.

He halted, staring at her. She sat motionless, just watching him back.

Hidy, she said.

Or he thought she said it. He heard it in his mind clear as a bell but he didn't know whether she had spoken or not. He hadn't seen her lips move, but he knew it was what she would have said had she spoken.

Hidy, Swaw said awkwardly.

Her face was pale in the waning sun, her gray eyes level and inscrutable. You got any drink on ye, Mr. Swaw?

With her knee hiked up like that he could see all the way up her dress, the white expanse of thigh and the blond hair at the juncture, the slightly parted flesh of her sex. She seemed not to mind his scrutiny.

Shore I got a drink. He reached her the halfpint bottle.

She unscrewed the cap and took a delicate drink, coughed a little, and shook her head. She handed it back.

You like that?

It's all right. I just like the way it makes me feel. Giddy and silly. The boys used to slip me a drink sometime. Drewry used to. It was a sight better whiskey than this, though. You know Drewry?

No.

I thought everybody knew Drewry. Drewry's all right. What are you lookin at?

I ain't lookin at nothin.

She laughed. The shit you ain't. You're lookin up my dress.

He looked away. A dark stain of twilight was seeping across the cornfield.

Stead of lookin at mine you ought to be studyin about some a little closer to home. You lettin them hogs of yourn run wilder'n a oneeyed jack, ain't ye?

I don't know.

Say you don't? You didn't catch one of em locked up there in the honeysuckles behind the woodshed? You ain't seen em playin that stinkfinger down below the spring there ever night?

Swaw drank from the bottle and shuddered.

A man do what he ought to do. He'd just lay around him with a shotgun and be done with it all, clean the whole nest of em out. Just be out of the whole mess.

———

He tried to shut it out of his mind, then something hard, a stick, struck him a vicious blow across the shoulders. He recoiled in pain. The girl cried out and writhed beneath him, her face, or his perception of it, altering, widening, the gray eyes darkening to a deep brown even as he watched in astonishment, the pale wisps of light hair at her temples coarsening and turning black until it was Retha's hair, Retha's face twisted beneath his own.

Oh sweet Jesus, he cried. He was abruptly sobbing raggedly. He pulled away from her and saw momentarily her white body sprawled on the quilts. Then his eyes whirled to see the hoehandle coming again, a demented and outraged Lorene swinging it. You bastard, she was saying over and over, spitting it at him. You bastard, you. The hoe caught him a glancing blow alongside the head. He threw up his arms to protect his face. His mouth was hurting already and all he could think of was the pain. He stumbled toward her, fending at the hoe, feeling it stinging against his arms.

His eyes fell on the ax. Before he knew what he was about he had grasped it up by the handle and sprung forward, buried it to the eye in her face, rocked it free of the bone automatically like a man splitting a cut of wood, and stood with it poised to fall again, looking down at her still body on the floorboards at his feet. A dark moonlit stain of blood crept toward him.

Daddy? Retha said. You coming back to bed?

Shut up, Swaw told her. Goddamn your soul to hell.

He walked out with the ax in his hand. He felt the cold dew on his feet, sweat drying on his body. He looked down and he was naked. The silver moon was above and behind him, wrought his shadow twisted and black as pitch, a moving recess to infinity he might stumble into.

He heard the door of the toolshed fall to. He looked back. She was standing naked in the wet grass watching him. Her eyes burned with a fierce luminosity. He turned and went on. He heard her following him, her feet scuffing softly in the grass.

A black dog came out of the tall weeds and sniffed at Swaw's tracks. A man stepped out of the shadows of the sycamore and stood leant against its bole watching him. A gangling black man came up from past the toolshed and followed him, his angular walk aping Swaw's dragfooted progress. The white man against the sycamore had long silver hair, muttonchop whiskers. Swaw did not notice. He went up the stone steps and into the dark recesses of the house.

Here pig pig pig, he called softly into the shadows. He went stealthily into the first bedroom he came to. The door creaked softly on its hinges. A pale yellow glow escaped as he pushed it open wide. Two here, rousing up at his step. He raised the ax. One scrambled up, fled past him, the other frozen dumb, mouth open. The last thing she saw was her naked father coming at her with the ax, its gleaming arc lit by the bare bulb of the nightlight.

He went out and sat on the stone steps and sobbed for a few moments. Then he couldn't remember why he was crying and ceased. The girl squatted in the wet grass watching him. She was all black and silver, white body gleaming like a beached fish stranded in the moonlight. The two men and the Mastiff were gone.

He wanted a drink. He felt for the bottle but he was naked and he couldn't for the life of him remember what he had done with his clothes.

He went into the bedroom to hunt them, found instead his shotgun leant in the corner and a cardboard box of shells sitting on the mantel. The box bore a picture of flying ducks. He took out two of the red waxed cylinders and loaded both barrels and went out again.

The shot that wounded one of his daughters brought the other out of the hall closet, arms outstretched and supplicant, shrieking. Swaw, cursing his luck and whirling after her, slipped in the slick blood and cracked his elbow on the floor. He struggled up, aiming on the fly at a frantic fleeing figure outlined against the moonlit yard. The explosion jarred his shoulder, blew off the top of her head and flung her limp as a rag doll through the screen and into the yard.

He went to reload. Images and memories flickered like frames of film in his mind: he couldn't remember his name but he could remember the girl's eyes, the serpent motionless below the screened lid, the way the crimped ends of the shotgun shells felt. The air smelled like cordite. A blue haze of smoke shifted dreamily beneath the hall ceiling.

She was heading for the steps, bloody from the wound, a hand held out to him. Daddy, she said. There was a petulant whine to her voice that he couldn't stand anymore. He shot her off the top step and turned the gun on himself, leaning down and taking the smooth, cold steel of the barrel into his mouth. He could see her white body against the black grass, limbs flung out and twisted as if she had fallen from some enormous height.

In his last attempt at coherent reasoning, Swaw figured he could fire the gun with his toe, and for once he was right.

Beale Station, 1982

He called Pauline from a payphone outside the 7-Eleven.

How much have you got?

Fifteen or twenty thousand words.

First draft or edited?

I don't know yet how much work I'll have to do on it.

And you're living down there, leased this place? Jesus, David. Can you afford that?

Well, I'm doing it. It's a gamble, I guess.

And it seems to me a wholly unnecessary one. Why did you have to live there to write a book about the place? Christ, you could have flown down and looked the place over, spent the night there if you had to. This living there, leasing or buying, it just seems...overkill, so unnecessary. I hope you never write a book about the Taj Mahal. I don't think that's for sale.

He felt inadequate, and he knew she was right. He could feel cold sweat along his sides, the beginnings of a headache, and for the first time a worm of doubt wriggled into his consciousness. He could see Corrie through the glass front of the market, and he wondered how long it would be until she was asking the same questions.

The book's coming along great. Anyway, I work better with my back against the wall. I get complacent if I'm not on the edge.

You'd know more about that than I would. But we're not talking about *Moby-Dick* here, or *Remembrance of Things Past*. All I suggested was a little thriller you could knock off to tide you over until you could get back to work on your novel.

I know that.

When can you send something along?

I'll try to get you three or four chapters and an outline in a week or so.

Whenever you can. If it's good enough maybe we can go for a quick paperback sale.

Pauline?

Yes?

I want you to find me a book. There's no way I can do it here, and New York City is the best place in the world to find an out-of-print book.

There was a pause, he guessed she was getting a pen and scratchpad.

Okay, what is it? Let's have it.

I don't know the title. The author's name sounds something like Sunderson, and he's a doctor of something. Probably a psychiatrist. The book is about the Beale haunting, and it'll probably have reference to that in the title.

If you need it, I'll do my damnedest. Do you know who published it, or when?

Or that it was, he thought to himself. No, he told her. It would have been about nineteen forty-four or forty-five.

All right. I'll try.

Thanks a lot.

He rang off and came out of the phone booth wringing wet with sweat into a day not much better. He hurried into the air-conditioned market.

You about ready?

More than. What did Pauline say?

She wants my typescript. She thinks she might sell it from an outline.

He got a six-pack of beer from the cooler, a *Playboy* and *Esquire* from the magazine rack, a tin of aspirin at the counter.

She drove, and he opened his shirt to the breeze, felt the wind drying the sweat to a glaze of salt, drank one of the beers ice cold and took three aspirin. They must have helped, for by the time they wound up the chert road home his headache was gone and he was thinking about the book again, blocking out the first scenes and planning what to begin typing.

She turned from putting away the groceries. You didn't say anything about my hair.

In fact he hadn't noticed it, but he said, I was just teasing you. It's very becoming. I like it.

Did you know that they actually have dances around here? Just a few miles down the road?

I didn't know that.

In a country schoolhouse that was closed when the county schools were consolidated. The Sinking Creek School. I'll bet it's real old. There's a band and everything, a fiddle player. A caller for the square dances.

In the living room Stephie had turned on the television set, put a videocassette of Winnie the Pooh into Binder's VCR. It sounds very nice, he told Corrie noncommittally.

I don't suppose you'd want to go, would you?

Tonight?

Well, yes, she said, knowing already that he wouldn't but not really disappointed, not really expecting it. After all, he was working, not sitting in a bar in Chicago drinking beer. The bills had to be paid. She was thinking about the videocassette recorder, too: one of David's seven-hundred-dollar toys. Where the money went.

I need to work tonight, Corrie. I have to do it when I can do it. I can't explain it to you. But I promise you I'll take you this summer. Do they have them every weekend?

I believe so. They were talking about it in the beauty shop. Will you really go?

Sure I'll go. It might be interesting. Binder hated dances but privately he thought he might be able to use it for the book, and if not this one for another. When he was working he always felt hypersensitive to stimuli, to things he ordinarily wouldn't even notice, and later in his manuscripts he would come across things that brought back moments of remembering, bits of conversation he had overheard, or simply the way someone had looked.

David?

He looked at her.

When we moved here, did you know that a man had murdered his family here and then killed himself?

No, I didn't. All I knew was the Beale legend. I heard about it in town today, but God's sake, Corrie, it was fifty years ago. What difference could it make?

None I guess, now. We're already here.

I'll tell you what I will do today. I'll take you swimming.

A real big spender, she said, smiling again.

With the remainder of the Cokes and a picnic basket of sandwiches, the three of them went down a footpath west of the house, came out on an old wagon road cut deeply into the earth, grown over with the lowering branches of enormous beech and sycamore, the road itself faint and vestigial, the ghost of a road. Off to the right was an area clear of underbrush, the earth mossy and damp, dark with shade broken by columns of light falling through the cathedrallike trees, the ground dappled with points of sun like strewn coins.

The haunted dell, he said.

What? She had dropped his hand.

Virginia Beale was called the Fairy Queen of the Haunted Dell. I think this is it.

She smiled at him, but a brief smile and one abruptly taken back.

You're always on, aren't you?

He shrugged. When I'm working, he said. Sorry. I always make the mistake of assuming the rest of the world is as interested as I am in what I'm working on.

You have a positively grotesque ego.

They came out of the bowered wood where the creek widened and deepened and a shelf of limestone rose out of the water, a table of rock fifteen or twenty feet long, the creek deep and bluelooking near the stone.

She ran ahead and waded out until her dark head vanished, only a forearm and waving hand showing, then surfaced, laughing and shivering, sleek hair plastered to her skull. She climbed onto the hot slab of limestone.

My God, it's icy, she said. I swear there are ice cubes floating in it.

He dove from the shallows and swam underwater across the pool, eyes open, the tabled rock floating past squared and geometric like some ancient structure hewn from stone. A rainbow trout turned in the sundrenched water, spun broken points of light at him. He rose toward the light, broke the glasslike surface of the water, dogpaddled to the shelf of rock.

Jesus, he said. It must be ten or twelve feet deep. And every bit as cold as you said.

He spread the beachtowel on the hot stone, lay back on it. This whole creek goes underground not a quarter mile from here, he said. It all roils around and funnels down into the ground. There's a big cylinder of rock with sides worn smooth as glass. It pours spewing down into the ground, and you can hear it churning around down in there. That's why they call it Sinking Creek.

You know a lot about this place for a novice.

I don't think I'm a novice anymore. I've covered a lot of ground around here in the last few days.

Exactly why escapes me.

Well, if you work at it, you've got to…take an interest.

She did not reply and he turned to study her face in repose, pillowed on a towel, her eyes closed, the sun throwing highlights of amber in her dark tousled hair. Delicate blue tracery of veins in her eyelids.

It's going to storm, he said suddenly. There was no response. Perhaps she slept. He turned to look at Stephie. She had waded out of the shallows, was gathering wildflowers on the far bank. Don't go in the woods, he told her.

Can I go just far enough to get those blue ones? she asked.

Go where it's clean, not where there's any undergrowth.

Okay.

Binder was watching Corrie's quiet face. This was the spot where the slaves used to have their baptizings, he said.

Used to what? she asked without opening her eyes.

Baptizings. The slaves had their meeting here, revivals I guess, and the preacher used to dunk them under to reclaim their souls. The Beale Haunt, or whatever she was, used to take quite an interest in the proceedings. She professed a great interest in religion. Washed in the blood, I guess. She used to sing and quote scripture to beat the band. She knew who was a sinner and who wasn't, and she used to show up every Sunday there was a meeting here and sort of supervise things. She used to yell out, Hold that nigger under a while longer, Preacher, he needs a double dose. Stuff like that.

You're making that up hand over fist, she said drowsily. Every last word of it, and it's not funny.

The hell I'm making it up. It's in the book. If you had read it when I was trying to get you to, you'd know I was telling you straight.

It was just boring to me. Besides, it doesn't matter. If you didn't make it up, somebody else did.

I guess so.

Banked clouds rose in the southwest, momentarily obscured the sun. Winds behind or inside them drove them, the smooth surface roiling on itself like the aftermath of an explosion, the blossoming of some grotesque flower. The world darkened and the woods grew greenblack. The air turned denser. He could see Stephie's bright head stooped to a flower in the glade. He kissed the hollow of Corrie's throat, freed her breasts from the bathing suit, the flesh around the nipple puckering with the cold touch of his hand. Here, here, she said sleepily. What are you doing? What kind of girl do you think I am?

He lay atop her body, feeling its heat, an urgency growing in him, with his hand between her legs, thinking: What is this? A warming of the cold war, a crack in the icemaiden's veneer. Past her upturned face he could see the far woods imbued with sudden motion, disappearing in a shifting curtain of rain, the weeds jerking under its weight as if swung toward them, the glass surface of the creek instantly cleft with myriad fractures, beginning to churn with the force of the rain, no longer blue but gray and alive with motion, some curious element forming in him.

There was only the green forest, the blue water, the bowl of blue sky to shelter them. No other in all the world. He made love to her gently, she with her eyes still closed, arms locked about his hips.

Hey, where are you going? she asked him. You weren't thinking of leaving, were you? This is much nicer than an umbrella.

Her hair was soaked, water swimming in his eyes. Jesus, what a cold rain, he said. He leapt up, hopping onelegged into his pants, pitched her the towel, began to gather the soap and hairbrushes, gave up on getting it all. The hell with it, he said, grabbing her arm, turning her toward the opening in the woods. He called to Stephie, who came with a fist full of flowers. Thunder boomed above them. Lightning lit the world in a harsh white bloom of light, vanished, drove them soaked and windhurried up the wagon road, the trees writhing above them like some mythic wood bewitched to momentary life, the running figures dollsized and furiously animate in the green wood, the air stiff and choked with leaves.

Something in him loved a storm. Once they were in dry clothes they sat beneath the tin roof of the porch and watched it pass over them and downstream, lightning arcing earthward from the band of clouds like tracerfire from some armada of smooth, metallic, otherworldly craft, thunder rumbling hollowly in the bottomland, the echo rolling back from the hills. Then the storm passed and the clouds lay broken behind it. The sun came out but already it lay on the horizon. It sank and a cool blue whippoorwill dusk lay on the land, broken only by the darkened trajectories of bullbats and a chorus of frogs from the creek.

He had set up a makeshift desk in the hall where there was a breeze from the screened-in backporch. After supper he typed for a while, vaguely aware of sounds of domesticities from the kitchen, conscious at once of the material he was working on and of her unseen presence beyond the kitchen wall. He could hear the whirring of the electric ice cream freezer. He was obscurely happy, drawing comfort from sourceless and insignificant things he always took for granted: the work he was doing, the soft worn feel of the faded jeans he was wearing, the sounds of the night beyond the walls, the feeling of the peace they engendered, the chaos of the world walled out.

They ate the ice cream on the stone doorsteps, touched by a sense of closeness without having to voice it. It had been a long day, an unhurried purposeless day Binder had stolen from the book, like a day he had managed to hoard from his childhood, squander when the mood suited him.

Later he would remember it as the last outpost of normalcy, a waystation to darker provinces.

Sometime in the night the wind arose again, but the house did not notice. Couched against the base of the hill and with its stone foundation laid on solid limestone, it had felt such storms for over a hundred years, had stood so while an incalculable number of winds rose and ebbed. It slept on. After a while it began to dream.

Binder halfawoke. A wind was banging a shutter somewhere, he could hear it slamming against the weather boarding. It was thundering off in the distance, and he could hear rain.

The bedroom door opened, closed softly, and he guessed the storm had awakened Corrie or that she had gone to the bathroom; he heard her bare feet cross the room, but instead of turning toward the side of the bed and climbing back in, she sat on the foot. He felt the mattress sink slightly beneath her weight, the faint protesting creak of the springs. She clasped the calf of his leg gently and he opened his eyes, lay for a moment in darkness until lightning abruptly lit the room and he saw that he was facing the tousled back of Corrie's head not four inches from his own.

Goddamn, he cried. He fairly leapt from the bed, ran across the room with his bare feet slapping the floor, whirling back when banked lightning in staccato progression showed the bed bare save the pale length of Corrie's naked body, the rumpled bedclothes.

He ran to Stephie's room, turned on the light. She was asleep with the covers thrown off, pajama-clad knees against her chest. He turned back the way he had come, went into the hall. He stood naked for a moment beneath the chandelier, confused and disoriented, looking wildly about the foyer, the staircases climbing incrementally into shadows.

A fierce bloom of light lit all the windows simultaneously with photoelectric brilliance, coincident to the boom of an explosion and Binder was sunk into oblivion. The silence there in the dark was enormous. It grew and expanded. He seemed deprived of all his senses save touch, sank to the floor. He could feel against his naked body the cold, smooth surface of floorcovering wet with rain driven through the open screen. The walls of the foyer seemed removed. He was lost in windy darkness, and the atmosphere of the house had changed, become profoundly malefic, as if the air had been charged by the switching on of some enormously evil battery.

Out of this silence came a feminine laugh, fey and whimsical, dry as the sound of cornshucks rustling together. The laugh rose in timbre, strangled itself instantly on a high gurgling note like the watervoiced call of a thrush. It was silent again.

I've got to get a hold of myself, Binder thought, but it took an enormous effort to remember his name. He sat waiting for the lights to come back on. They did not. The goddamned transformer, he thought, remembering the explosion. He tried to recall what he had done with the flashlight: the nightstand drawer. He arose, felt his way cautiously toward the wall until lightning mapped the room. He made the bedroom door, paused again, gained the wall in darkness, and felt along it until the room was briefly lit.

The flashlight was there. He snapped it on and felt better immediately. He looked at Corrie. He didn't know how, but still she slept. He hesitated by the door of Stephie's room, loath to turn and go, but ultimately the thought of someone else in the house was intolerable. There was no way he was going to get back to sleep. He wished the gun had been unpacked. Binder was trying not to think about the hand on his leg.

He was halfway up the stairs when the singing began. Vague, far-off, murmurous, no words he could decipher and maybe no words at all, maybe just the voice filtered through the walls and time and his consciousness, the melody familiar and curiously nostalgic, timeless. He thought desperately of songs he knew, anything to drown out the hypnotic song. The Beatles, he thought, think of the Beatles, listen to the music playing in your head.

He was on the landing, and the music had grown clearer, louder in volume. A feminine voice, a contralto, innocent and pure, a young girl's voice.

He couldn't understand the words yet. The beam of the flashlight played about the upstairs hall. All he could hear was the rasp of his own breathing. The singing was coming from behind a closed mahogany door. Cheek laid against it, he could feel the smooth, cold wood and hear the woodfiltered voice singing still.

He threw open the door. It was empty save a bed, a functional-looking chest of drawers. Silent, too, for the singing had stopped at the opening of the door as surely as if he had jerked the tone-arm of a phonograph off a record, cut off instantly in midnote.

He could hear, rising above the silence, the wash of rain at the uncurtained windows. Turning with the light he saw only his reflection and the glassed-out silver motion of water. The air of the room felt electric and telluric, as if it had just been quit by the presence of another.

The singing commenced in the next room. Sweet, a capella, for some reason it made him think of a young girl at her toilet, preening before a mirror, singing softly to herself.

He turned with the light, crept stealthily into the hall, approached the bedroom door, twisted the knob gently. Abruptly he kicked the door so hard it slammed against the wall, played the light desperately over the room. Now the singing was behind him, descending the stair, and he began to understand the words:

> Lay down, my dear sister
> Won't you lay and take your rest
> Won't you lay your head upon your Savior's breast?
> And I love you, but Jesus loves you the best
> And I bid you goodnight...goodnight...goodnight

He descended the stairs two at a time, but the voice had turned a corner in the hall. Shining the light toward the corner he saw for an instant the hindquarters of a black dog. He ran toward it, the light bobbing from ceiling to floor, rounded the corner into the kitchen and swept the light from side to side.

Nothing.

The singing was faint and far off, indecipherable. A man's hoarse and guttural voice abruptly said something. It might have been curse or invocation. The singing rose in timbre. The man's voice began again, singsong, a nursery rhyme, patient and slow, as if laboriously explaining something to a child.

A is for ark, that wonderful boat
Noah built it on land getting ready to float.

Silence then except the singing.
The man said patiently,

B is for beast at the ending of the wood, who ate
    all the children
When they wouldn't be good.

The voice slurred drunkenly off into an incoherent mumble.

Above the voices Corrie was calling David, David, a rising voice verging on panic.

The lights came on. The refrigerator compressor kicked in, began to hum reassuringly. He could hear the air conditioner whirring from the bedroom. The atmosphere of the house altered, seemed drained of evil.

She was sitting on the side of the bed, a blanket across her lap, hands cupping her breasts defensively, eyes wide with alarm until she recognized him.

Where were you, David?

Looking for something…I heard something.

Heard something? What? Why was it dark, was the power off?

I guess lightning knocked it out and they fixed it. I heard something walking…the door was open. I guess it was a dog.

A dog, she said in disbelief.

She said something else, but Binder did not hear. He checked on Stephie then lay down on the bed. The sheets were damp and cool, the air conditioner was drying the sweat on him. His head hurt. He closed his eyes, aware of her beside him, but he was thinking of the cool hand on his calf, the aching purity of the

voice. He wondered at which point his fear had turned to exul-
tance and he was remembering Charlie Cagle on the park bench
saying, You let such as that in your own self. Somehow he had
done that, and the thought of his own complicity in it was more
frightening than the singing had been.

An Excerpt from *The Beale Haunting*
by J. R. Lipscomb

Jacob Beale was born in 1785 in Halifax County, Virginia. He was the eldest son of Henry Beale, a wealthy landowner and planter of English and Irish descent. For over a hundred years the Beales had been a wellknown English family.

He was educated to the standards of those primitive times, going to school in the wintertime and the rest of the year being trained in the management of the Beales' lands, and proved to be an exceptional pupil, for almost immediately he began to prosper in the manner of his father and of Beales before him.

In 1809 he began to court a young woman named Elizabeth Anne Cotton. The Cottons were also a highly thought of family, being of good stock and acquisitive of possessions as befits those who would build an empire from a virgin wilderness. In the standards of the time, Miss Cotton had many other admirers, being most comely and healthy, stout enough to be an admirable helpmate, an attribute not to be taken lightly in those harsh times. She was known as Becky to these suitors, and widely sought after.

But the Beales, as has been said, were an important family in Halifax County and young Jacob the most eminent bachelor, and when his heart bade him seek the hand of Becky Cotton he did so with the same unreserved determination that he used in his business pursuits, and all opposition fell before him, so that they were married in October of that year.

The Cottons were most gratified to welcome young Beale into the bosom of their family. They presented as a dowry a young Negro man named Vestal and a good stout Negress called Chloe, as well as several good head of livestock and sundry other items of value.

The newly married Beales built a house on a part of Henry Beale's holdings, and for some twenty years Jacob continued his duties as overseer of the family lands, during which time he continued to prosper materially as well as in other ways, nine children being born to him, six of whom survived: Jacob Jr., Elizabeth, Anne, Sewell, Drewry, and the baby, daughter Virginia, comely from birth and from all accounts the apple of Jacob's eye. She was flaxenhaired and blue-eyed, named for the good Virginia soil that had so abetted her father's continued enrichment.

Chloe, the slave woman, was extremely fertile as well, presenting him with eight children, all of whom lived and were healthy, eventually maturing and breeding and adding to the wealth he was accumulating.

The only cloud on Mr. Beale's horizon was that about 1830 his wife developed some type of female affliction that prevented the birth of further children, and from all accounts prevented the Beales from having a normal husband-and-wife relationship.

He was a most thrifty man, extremely close with his money, so that it surprised many when he bought a parcel of land in Tennessee and prepared to move, but he did so in the face of malicious rumors that surfaced and were spread. There had been hints of heinous deeds, most certainly unfounded and probably born out of the jealousy the deprived must feel for those who gather about them effortlessly the trappings of material wealth, and one need only peruse the affidavits signed by the men who knew Jacob Beale in his lifetime and witnessed his persecution at the hands of the Haunt to recognize immediately the forthrightness and candor of his nature.

The most persistent of these innuendos made reference to a scandal involving an itinerant traveling preacher and his young sister. This preacher was a worshiper of the serpents he used in his services, and his sister, possessing an affinity for the snakes, tended them. In the fall of 1837 the preacher came to Halifax County and, for a sum of money, was allowed to set up his tent on the Beale land.

Within the week the nude body of the young girl was found in the woods near the Beale holdings, strangled and assaulted in a manner whose description would appeal only to the prurient. Probably for reasons of blackmail, the preacher accused Jacob Beale, claiming that he had seen his little sister strolling into the woods with Beale a day or two before the body was discovered. He went so far as to swear out warrants and cause them to be served, but before the matter could be brought before a grand jury the preacher himself disappeared, most everyone supposing that he had grown afraid of the consequences when his ruse was discovered, others assuming that he might have committed the atrocious act himself.

However base and unfounded these stories might have been, they could be part of the reason Beale departed Virginia. For whatever reason, in 1838 he came to Tennessee and purchased a 1,600-acre tract of land in the Sinking Creek area of Limestone County, an area recently moved to by some of Mr. Beale's friends. The house on the place was one of the best in the state at that time, being a large log dwelling two stories high and weatherboarded with cedar.

Immediately the Beales began to improve their new holdings, planting a large orchard between the road and the house and clearing the thick timber away for new grounds, the logs serving as building material for slavequarters and for other outbuildings, as well as a great barn that remains standing today, though the original house has been torn down and a larger one built some distance away.

In those days neighbors helped one another with their tasks, there being log rollings and barn raisings and cornhuskings. These communal endeavors, as well as attendance at church, which neared one hundred percent, served to engender a closeness among these people.

Jacob Beale almost immediately caused a schoolhouse to be built and hired a schoolteacher, paying the first year's salary out of his own pocket. This alone should serve to refute the lies about Mr. Beale's stinginess. Though he was sometimes harsh in his dealings and forthright in his needs, he was never less than honest, and during years when his neighbors failed to prosper, through bad luck or ill weather, he was not averse to loaning them money until their own conditions improved. Such improvement was not always the case, however, and over the years the Beale holdings increased due to defaulted notes and mortgages.

In these first years in Tennessee, before being afflicted by the Haunt, Mr. Beale entered into the spirit of the community, though he was of a stern and religious nature and not given to frivolities such as dancing and strong drink, which he thought of as sinful.

On the eve of the haunting, Virginia was fourteen and Elizabeth and Jacob Jr. were married, having become betrothed to members of the community and built their homes on one-hundred-acre tracts their father granted them. Life seemed to have fallen into a pattern of content, and Jacob Beale must have contemplated happily the tapestry that the loom of life was weaving for him; he would have been less than human had he not. He had a large, healthy family that had never hungered for food or shelter, sons and daughters who were marrying well, Elizabeth marrying a young sawmill owner named Zadok Kirk and Jacob Jr. taking as his bride Julia Primm, the daughter of the Baptist preacher Joseph Primm, who will recur in the narrative at a later time.

Drewry was at an impressionable age when the haunting began, and he was so afflicted by the things he saw the Haunt do to his father and sister that he never married, living his entire life in the fear of the monster's predicted return and never allowing during his lifetime the publications of any of his journals, though huge sums of money were offered by various national periodicals. Virginia Beale became known in the national press as the Queen of the Haunted Dell, and received worldwide attention in the press, as clippings from newspapers in London, England, attest.

As to the nature of the haunting, the phenomenon in question was referred to as the Haunt, for want of a better term. The Haunt was invariably called "she," owing to her feminine voice, notwithstanding the obscenities it spoke.

Life passed uneventfully for the first two or three years in Tennessee. Jacob Beale and his family were by all accounts well thought of and admired by their neighbors, and Jacob became an important factor in the local elections. Possessing a fine speaking voice and being a large, handsome man with a fine head of curly grey hair, he cut an impressive figure in his splittail coat and beaver hat when his many business dealings drew him to Memphis or Nashville.

At fourteen, pretty blueeyed Virginia Beale, or Ginny, was already sought after by local swain, one of her suitors being Thomas Campbell, the schoolteacher her father had hired. Another was Eulis Varner, a likable local boy of great promise.

At the time their family trouble began (Drewry referring to it thusly in his journals), she was gay and carefree, nothing ahead of her but the unbroken serenity of her future, playing with her brothers and sister in the surrounding woods and learning by heart all the names of the birds and wildflowers, making pets of the rabbits and young deer with which the forest abounded, and secure in the love of a doting father.

One day Jacob walked over his fields to see how his crops were faring, as harvest time was nigh and the weather critical. He was walking across the field toward his overseer, Vestal, when he stopped to stare at an unusual black animal watching him from a corn middle. The animal looked like a dog, but of a breed Mr. Beale was not familiar with; it was high in the shoulders and had a long, snoutlike mouth.

He had his gun with him, the slaves having reported snakes about the place, and the peculiar fixity of the beast's eyes so perturbed Mr. Beale that he aimed and fired. The dog appeared to fall but then vanished and left no trace.

Ginny claimed to have seen a woman strolling in the orchard, wringing her hands and crying, who beckoned to her and called her by name. Having no reason to suspect that the figure was other than flesh and blood, and possessed of a concern for the woman's apparent grief, Ginny approached, only to see her vanish in the summer twilight.

Drewry shot at a great brown bird, a bird such as none of them had ever seen. It alighted one dusk in an enormous cedar with a great flapping of its wings, and it was of such a malevolent appearance that his first thought was to destroy it. Drewry was one of the finest marksmen in the county, being generally the winner of all the turkey shoots and bird hunts, but though the bird seemed to drop from the cedar he could find not so much as a feather to attest the trueness of his shot, and was wont to blame his poor aim on the failing light of dusk.

There was much work to do that fall, and Jacob Beale, with many slaves to supervise and all the crops to gather, with the attendant sorghum-making and woodcutting for winter, putting up of food and also of grain for the animals, gave all these events short shrift.

As has been said, he was by nature a most stern and pragmatic man, and even severely reprimanded Ginny, by all accounts his favorite. According to Drewry's journal, he told them, relenting a little his severity, that in Tennessee there were many fowl and animals strange to them, that they were seeing normal animals and attaching the trappings of superstition.

The winter, a harsh one with many snows, seemed to have passed uneventfully, the Beales reporting nothing out of the way, though Vestal swore he saw a light bobbing about the winter cornfields and that on the way to visit his wife, who lived at a neighboring farm, he habitually met a black dog in the same spot of the road every night, no matter what time his progress brought him to that point.

Then in the early spring, when the trees were greening out, Ginny was on her way home from school when she chanced to look down into a meadow that bordered the path she was on. There was a great oak tree there where the children used to play, and swinging from one of its topmost branches was a young girl. The girl wore a dress of brown homespun, a butternut color, and she had long yellow hair like Ginny, who did not recognize her and drew nearer to call to her, thinking her new to the neighborhood and not yet entered in school.

The girl was watching her, holding the limb by her arms and swinging slowly in the air. Ginny crossed the splitrail fence and stooped to put down her books, and when she looked up the girl was gone. The branch still tossed with released weight.

From that the haunting grew in intensity, as if it drew nourishment from the fecund growth of that long-ago wilderness spring, or had some urgent need to make itself known so strongly that even Jacob Beale himself could no longer deny its existence.

Noises began to be heard at night, soft and furtive, so that the Beale family felt the house had become infested with rats; during the night gnawing sounds would issue forth until it seemed that the very beds were being consumed as they lay upon them, and there was a persistent chewing behind the paneling, but when lights were lit and carried from room to room nothing seemed to have been disturbed.

There were the sounds of dogs fighting, as if chained together to battle to the death, bounding and leaping over the furniture. One night a great flapping of wings in the attic that moved from one corner to the other, as if some winged beast the size and weight of a heifer calf was cavorting there.

During the day the Beales would ransack the house from top to bottom, some of the flooring and paneling even being removed and replaced in an effort to locate the source of their troubles, all of which was in vain. Cats and dogs were brought into the house at nightfall to try and scent out the infestation, the animals behaving peculiarly and immediately seeking an egress; no dog ever spent the night willingly in Jacob Beale's house after the haunting began. This was tried early and abandoned, as the dogs created such a cacophony of noise with their howling and whimpering, not ceasing even when Jacob Beale arose to beat them, that the family seemed almost to prefer the sounds of the Haunt.

These were trying times for the Beales, and though they could not have known it, they were to continue for four more years.

Jacob Beale was a man trying to get a crop in and keep his slaves under control, who were likewise affected by the haunting. Ignorant and superstitious, they were even more terrorized by the sounds and flitting lights than the white people were, some of them even slipping away and trying to escape, having to be returned by patrollers. Mr. Beale was under great pressure at this time, as were to a lesser degree the members of his family. Unable to sleep at night and having to carry on his business and financial transactions in the daytime, he now became afflicted by a singular malady. His tongue and jaws seemed to be most affected, swelling and paining him so intensely that he was at times unable to speak or eat. These spells were generally of short duration, however, enabling him to continue his business affairs rather than completely giving up and taking to his bed.

At first he tried to blame the nocturnal noises on the effects of the earth quaking, earthquakes being on the mind of Tennesseans, a severe quake having just recently struck Tennessee, affecting much of the countryside and creating Reelfoot Lake, which at that time was widely believed to be bottomless.

At last, however, he was forced to seek outside help, going for counsel to Brother Joseph Primm, preachers being known to possess a greater knowledge of such things than the common man.

It is not recorded what Brother Primm thought of these revelations, but he and his wife agreed to spend the night with the Beales and listen for themselves. Before retiring he offered a prayer and a song, praying piously and at great length for the good Lord to direct his attentions toward alleviating the circumstances that had brought his friend Beale to such a sorry state.

The lights were scarcely blown out and the folk abed before the Haunt seemed to fairly spread herself. Objects were thrown, the sound of furniture being overturned, the covers were jerked from Brother Primm's fingers. For the first time coarse and derisive laughter arose, went effortlessly from room to room, and continued so loudly that none were able to sleep, not even desisting when Reverend Primm called loudly on a Higher Power, but continuing until it seemed to tire itself out, or just to weary of the game.

The next day, under the advice of Brother Primm, others of Jacob's neighbors were told of the troubles, the affair being of so complicated a nature that the efforts of their common minds might be able to unravel this riddle.

They were sworn to secrecy, but in a community as small and closely knit as Sinking Creek, and a matter as marvelous as this one was, it can come as no surprise that word spread throughout the countryside like wildfire, so that in the evenings the house would be full of neighbors who had gathered to hear for themselves these wonders.

Reverend Primm was the unofficial leader of the group, and he used to sit before the fire and talk to the Haunt, beseeching it to speak and make its purpose known. To their great surprise it did learn to talk, making at first a kind of babylike gurgling. As the nights passed it grew stronger, saying a few words and humming a few lines from gospel songs of that day; and then one night it began to speak, repeating word for word Reverend Primm's sermon of the previous Sunday, and concluding with the song he had used to lead the service. It was a wonderful mimicry, copying perfectly the inflections of Brother Primm's mellifluous voice.

As soon as the Haunt could speak it was begged to reveal its intentions, and it was not loathe to do so. It said that it had come to torture Virginia Beale and to drive Jacob Beale, whom it referred to as old Jake, to his death, at which time it promised to return whence it had come.

After crops were laid that summer, they would be there every night. The yard would be full of wagons and tethered horses, playing children chasing fireflies, solitary workers appearing sourceless in blue dusk from whichever direction they happened to live in. Not even waiting now for full dark, but stringing out along the roads in early dusk, whole families of them coming from God knew where, folks Beale had never seen before or heard rumored, the men dressed in their Sunday best, stiff on the wagon seats, the women bonneted in their best finery, shifting the snuffstick aside in their drawstring mouths and watching him with their flinty little eyes, knowing as sure as death that he knew what they came to hear: not the gospelsinging or the sugarmouthed pseudopreaching but the Haunt's obscene rantings, its dirtymouth tattling of the community doings. Them hearing it and rolling their eyes in spurious shock and saying, They Lord have mercy, as if it had taken them by surprise, as if it was not something they had come anticipating, by now a perverse source of entertainment that drew them gapejawed and slackmouthed out of the brush as sugar draws flies.

And him feeding them, likely as not. Or having to offer, anyway, a few of them saying no thanks ye, we got a little somethin here we brought. The rest of them taking whatever fare was offered, and there would have to be more flour and coffee brought by the end of the month.

Standing there in the hall of the haysmelling barn dappled with moted light, he estimated the number of horses, said to himself, How about a pad of hay for my horses, Brother Beale? Or two pads, or an armful of corn.

Yet he watched with more than cynicism. He studied these outlanders, neighbors, halffools and wholefools. There might be the one man who would study this chaos with a bright and unjaundiced eye and say, as if it were something they should have noticed long ago, why here's the trouble right here, leant to study the situation like a man indicating the fault in a haymower that would not work.

He watched his sons cross the field with the horses, angle along toward the creek to water them. Dusk drew on. Lights were lit in the house. Soon he would be expected to put in an appearance, to exchange civilities with his neighbors, with these strangers who'd come to amuse themselves at his expense, and say you're from where? My land, that's a far piece, and you come all the way by wagon. Their eyes asking each other, how does he do it anyway? And why does he?

He waited, loathe to leave here for the tobacco smoke–scented front room, the turbulent emotional atmosphere from which the Haunt drew strength. Here he could smell the placid animals that he had come to respect more than men, the hay that reminded him of the last days of summer.

The blondehaired girl in a green dress sat by the fireplace. She sat in a willow rocker, unmoving, her hands in her lap. Her eyes were closed; perhaps she slept. Yet every eye in the crowded room was upon her. The people jammed into the room and seated on ladderbacks and kitchen chairs or just hunkered against the wall seemed not to breathe. What's the matter with her? She's subject to the vapors. The girl's color was high, cheeks lit by a mottled red blush, and her breathing was harsh and irregular, could be heard from the farthest corner of the room.

Joseph Primm began to pray, kneeling on the floor, bracing himself against the hearth of the dead fireplace, speaking of theft, of the value a man attached to his personal belongings, of the roiling flames of hellfire awaiting the man who took this value lightly.

The girl had not moved. She slept on. Beside her sat an old black woman with a fan, moving it listlessly, the faint breeze moving in the pale tendrils of flaxen hair at the temples.

At last Primm ceased. A sigh of creaking chairs, a general hum of coughing and throatclearing. A few began to talk about stealing. Things they had taken from them.

I was never one to hold with stealin, a man from Jack's Branch said boldly. But I reckon if a man was starvin to death and took a little grub the Lord would take that into consideration. It don't seem right for a man to burn in hell forever for stealin a bite to eat.

How long'd it take you to eat that horse you stole in South Carolina? a voice shot back instantly. The voice seemed to come from the far corner of the ceiling and every head in the room turned, the necks twisting like some synchronous machine.

I never stole no horse, the man cried.

You're a goddamned liar. You never stole a chestnut gelding from a man named Burbank and sold it in Town Creek, Alabama?

The voice was at once sourceless and omnipresent, seeming to shift its position, as if it feared to remain in one place too long: rising and falling, a soft feminine voice, sweet and innocent, a dream voice, a voice like no other they had heard in all their lives.

I never took no horse, the man said stubbornly to his neighbor.

Hell, the other said, wryly amused, don't tell me. I never said you did.

After a while the man left. He would not be the first that night, but the voice had lost interest, began to hum to itself some old gospel song. Come to the church in the wildwood, breaking the song off, childlike, as if its attention span were short.

Where's old Jake? it wondered abruptly. Where's Jake Beale? Is he not in here? Where is that whorechasing old smellsmack?

The voice ceased, as if counting heads, searching among all those present.

Mr. Beale is not here, Joseph Primm said. He's taking care of the livestock.

Oh he is, is he? I know the livestock Mr. Beale has his mind on, Sugarmouth. He's peeping at those courting couples playing a little stinkfinger out in the edge of the woods…is Virginia here? That thicklegged little slut, is she here? She likes to play that stinkfinger too. I saw her and Mr. Posey down by the springhouse a night or two ago…he had her dress wadded up around her waist and his finger up in her and Lord, how she loved it.

The room was struck by a delirious hush of silence. In the back of the room a woman had arisen haughtily, her face a haggard mask of contempt.

She never played it, the voice said, her leaving there. She never had one in her, not in a day or two anyway. She's like Sugarmouth there, he don't know what stinkfinger is. Do you, Sugarmouth? He doesn't. He thinks it's something like tiddlywinks, but Virginia doesn't. Virginia thinks it's much nicer than that, don't you, Virginia? Sugarmouth doesn't know anything about such worldly things, he doesn't even lope his mule behind the barn anymore.

The voice babbled on mindlessly, rising and falling like a madman talking to himself.

Why do you carry on such crazy filth? Primm asked earnestly. You have a fine mind, a great knowledge and memory of the Bible. You could move countless souls toward heaven. Your singing could move thousands of lost sheep into the folds of Christianity.

Don't you just love the way old Sugarmouth talks? The voice was fey and whimsical. Don't you just wish you could go home and talk that way too, whenever you wanted? I know I do. But Sugarmouth's not very smart. He thinks it's me. It's not me, Sugarmouth. I'm…I'm everything and nothing…. Here the voice faltered, trailed weakly off, struggled with a thought, a concept or the way to express one. I'm just a mirror, Sugarmouth. All I can do is reflect what you bring me. You give me a roomful of Christians and I'll give you back Christianity. These folks here, though…

She's doin it, a man said suddenly. That whiteheaded gal's makin it talk somehow.

Sewell Beale was watching with indolent, sleepy eyes. He was sitting backward in a canebottom chair, his arms laced across the top slat, his bootheels hooked in the rounds. He was a young man with long dirtyblond hair. His eyes were hooded and chill. His upper lip was covered by a soft blond mustache. You're talking about my sister, sir, he said coldly, and you are doing it in her house. Say one more word and you will answer to me outside, and you be required to furnish more than your mouth to do it with.

The man arose awkwardly. I forgit where I am, he said. I apologize.

Beale nodded coldly in dismissal.

The black woman had laid aside her fan. Every eye in the room watched alike. Her movements had something of ceremony, intuition, a ritual performed many times before. She clasped the girl's mouth, the fingers of each hand overlapping over her lips. The girl didn't stir. The silence stretched, elongated. The audience sat hypnotically rapt.

It would serve the little bitch right if I kept my peace, the voice mused, altering, taking on a selfsatisfied tone. The old black woman sat still as ebony statuary. Then what you do? the voice asked. Band together, tar and feather her, I suppose, and it would be no more that she deserves, the little spreadlegged beast…but do you actually think I'm something she dreamed up to pass the time? I'm more than that.

Then just what sort of monster are you? Primm asked it.

I'm no kind of monster. I am greater than the God you pray to, less than the spittle of a dog's tongue. I have been here forever, and I will be here when the worms have long finished with you. Now, what kind of monster are you?

That's no kind of answer at all.

Do you want me to lie to you? I remember what I told old Jake one time…Old Jake was whiteeyeing on me, laying down, he finally knew I was going to stay till I killed him…he kept asking what I was (here the voice changed, coarsened, took on the unmistakable timbre of Jacob Beale's voice)…Why are you so set on torturing me? What have I ever done to deserve such treatment?

The voice shifted eerily, became curiously neutral, a voice without sex or accent. I said, well, Old Jake, I was one of the first settlers in these parts and I was attacked and killed by Indians here sixty years ago, and I was buried right where your front porch is. When they were building this house, they dug up my grave and reburied the bones down below your spring. They left one of my fingerbones there where the grave was and my soul won't ever rest in peace till I get a decent burial. Well, Old Jake got them boys humpin. They tore up the floorboards and they was digging up dirt and siftin it lookin right and left for that lost fingerbone. It was in July, and Lord it was hot. After about half a day, I got to feelin sorry for them boys and I broke down and told em I was just sportin with em.

Old Jake still didn't believe me. He took a grubbin hoe and shovel and dug up that whole bottom there lookin for a grave. Of course he never found one, but anyway that old reprobate did the only full day's work he ever did.

The voice went on and on without ceasing or even an intimation of ceasing, abusive, obscene, vituperate, until Jacob Beale bolted into the front yard, the door slamming to behind him, opening and closing with the passage of no visible person and the voice commencing again immediately. Beale halfrunning blindly across the frozen yard into the silver moonlight past the dark bulk of the trees.

Run, goddamn you, the voice shrieked. Anywhere you go I'll be there and waiting for you.

Sewell Beale came onto the porch. Father, he called.

He crossed the yard and took the old man's arm. Come in by the fire, he said.

Come in by the fire, the voice mimicked. Don't you worry about Old Jake. He'll be in the fire soon enough.

There was the flat sound of a slap and Beale's head lurched sidewise, the long silver hair fanning out, his eyes wide and horrified. More blows, methodical, first on one cheek and then the other, his head jerking crazily from side to side. He tried to run, turning, his left foot dragging on the frozen ground, and then fell as if from a blow across the back of the head. Sewell Beale was flailing at the air, cursing, trying at once to grasp whatever it was and to shield his father. He could feel the blows falling across his own shoulders, sharp measured blows from a stick or walking cane, making a twack, twack on the heavy wool overcoat.

My shoes, boy, the old man said, and Sewell looked, still feeling the stinging blows across his shoulders. He watched his father's boots unlacing themselves, the rawhide thongs writhing out of the eyelets as if magically invested with life, crawling out.

He could hear maniacal laughter above him. He grasped the boots, one on his father's foot. No sooner was he at the one than the other was jerked off. He lashed the lacing round the cuff of the boot and felt the boot slide from beneath it. The heel of the boot caught him hard on the temple and he lay for a moment dazed, his cheek pillowed against the cold ground. His father's feet had begun to jerk eerily as if performing some demented buck-and-wing, kicking madly at the air until Sewell stopped them with his weight, felt them still moving spasmodically against his belly, the flesh of his father's face contorted, dancing as if every nerve had been divested of coherent purpose, left with only uncontrolled twitching.

The laughter died away. The old man grew still. Sewell saw his eyes were wide with fear and incomprehension, tears forming there and welling over the sockets. Son, the old man awkwardly began, his voice breaking off. Son, she.... There seemed to be little of his father left in this pathetic old man.

There were tears in his own eyes now, and Sewell wiped them away with the rough sleeve of the coat. He didn't say anything. It was far too quiet. There was only the cold wind in the distance, the frozen trees keening over the bare winter fields. He helped Beale up, put his shoes on and tied them. This time they stayed tied. Come on, he said. The old man stood stubborn and disoriented, looking toward the single light flaring in the house, looking out across the fogbound fields as if all places were the same to him.

Come on, Sewell said again, tugging at his arm. The old man came reluctantly, his left foot dragging audibly over the whorled earth.

Where?

The barn. We're hitching up a team and leaving. I'm taking you and Mama over to Jacob Junior's.

It won't do any good.

How do you know what'll do good?

I just know.

Sudden anger flared in Sewell, fierce and violent. Anger at the old man for his stoic acceptance, anger at the horror that had consumed his father and sister, that might in his turn consume him until he lay in his grave. All right, by God, he said. Then we won't go to Jacob's. We'll go to Virginia, or Carolina, or Kentucky. Sell the hellhole or give it away, if you could find a taker like you could have done four years ago, if you hadn't been too damn stingy to take a penny's loss.

Halfway to the barn he turned at a sound. A figure had stepped from the darkness pooled in the orchard and strolled silently along, pacing them through the stalks of winter weeds on the other side of the fencerow, gliding toward convergence at the end of the pasture. He hurried the old man, not even hearing the mumbling complaint, his stomach icy with dread. He'd thought his belief was suspended, that he could accept anything without fear, but each manifestation had the quality of being marvelously new yet the same at the core, old wine in new bottles he thought, so that each time his reason was assaulted anew.

He looked back. The figure was climbing the wooden stockgate, a figure in a long gray or black dress. The woman was in motion, climbing down then jumping the last two or three feet to land soundlessly in the roadbed, silhouetted for a moment, inkblack against the paler heavens: its face was long and cowshaped, he could see the hooked horns curving out from the sides of the head.

Come on, he said, panic running through him. He pulled the old man's wrist, Beale halfrunning in a sort of lurching shuffle. He could hear the cattle then, smell them, the clean summer-smelling hay.

He looked back. There was nothing, the wooden stockgate silhouetted against the sky, stark and austere. The road lay brimming with moonlight, cold and white and empty.

———

The girl moaned softly, stirred in the willow chair. The black woman had a hand to her forehead. Virginia opened her eyes, which were for a moment depthless and blue and profoundly devoid of expression, then in an instant congested with bewilderment, confusion. She clasped the black woman's arm and her face seemed to calm, as if she drew comfort from the old slave through some acute sensation of touch.

What did she say, Chloe? she asked. Did I miss her talking tonight?

Beale Station, Summer 1982

The weekends were the worst, Corrie thought. The weekdays were not so bad—David had been used to working at some job during the weekday, writing in the evenings. That was the way it had been in Chicago, and he still seemed locked into this pattern, unable to write until the afternoon drew on. So he would wander amiably about the place, talk to her, help around the house, assist her time in its arduous flight, always seeming restless, waiting, ill at ease, but still *there*, anyhow, not like weekends.

Saturday morning he would begin as if freed from a forty-hour workweek and continue through the day and night until exhaustion forced him to cease, giving up the notebook or typewriter with visible reluctance.

Even then he was still working. He would be wound too tight, distant and vague, his mind numb, she thought, as he glanced occasionally at her in a curious, speculative manner that disturbed her, as if wondering who she was, how she fitted into the scheme of things. If she spoke to him he would answer her cordially enough, but he didn't volunteer anything. He'd just sit on the end of the sofa, legs crossed, a cigarette burning unattended in his fingers, his eyes heavylidded, inwardlooking. His mind, she guessed, still filled with the people that were realer to him than she could ever be. Even though she always read his work, the simple reading of it did not carry her where he had been.

And the worst part of it was that she had thought this book was to be different; in the writing of his other two novels he had been dealing with real people in life-and-death situations, concerned with tying together the disparate threads of his characters' lives, almost unable to let them go. Now he was supposed to be knocking off a ghost story for the money and forgetting it, taking a little time off then getting on to more serious things. Secretly she had thought that was the idea that he just let be, she thought he had the ability that this would squander. They should have just tightened their belts and made do, they could have made it until the second book was made publishable, been more thrifty with the little money they got and not spent what they had on a ruined backwoods mansion.

Sunday afternoon was more of the same, hot and clear and a mile long. The steady clack clack clack of the typewriter ceasing only when he paused to light a cigarette, make coffee, go to the bathroom. She was counting the days till Labor Day.

She wished she had brought gardening tools. The yard was flanked with tall brick flowerbeds, she guessed all that was left of the sisters Abernathy. There were peonies, bloodred cannas, others she didn't even recognize, all of them strangling in weeds and crabgrass.

She began to pull weeds, turning their roots to die in the sun, planning on next Saturday already and it only being Sunday: fertilizer and small hoe, a trowel to loosen the earth about the flowers. Maybe he'd go before Saturday. Maybe they'd run out of something.

The earth was parched and hard, solid as clay baked in the sun. The stick she prodded it with broke and she pitched it aside and arose, wiping her hands on her shorts.

She turned. The toolshed. There would be something, even if it was only a sharp piece of steel. She could loosen the soil and water the cannas; it was better than Sunday evening TV.

Serried gloom within, slats of white sunlight where the shakes were missing from the roof. She stood for a moment, letting her eyes adjust to the shadows. Oddments of unidentifiable junk, scrapiron, old broken purposeless tools took shape out of the plasmic shade.

It was hot in the shed, the air still and lifeless, freighted with nearinvisible motes of dust turning like spinning points of light. The smell of hot wood baking in the sun, the dank odor of moldy earth. Slow sleepy drone of insect wings. She looked up. Above the door wasps were flying about an enormous gray paper nest, arriving, departing, involved in some commerce known only to themselves, ugly red wasps thick as her little finger. She looked away, glanced about for anything that looked as if it would serve her purpose.

A wooden platform covered half the earth floor, as if, she thought, the toolshed had once been floored and then part of it had been ripped up. The wooden bins, she figured, had held foodstuffs, perhaps potatoes, bags of dried beans. Against the wall, amidst a motley of thrownaway clothes, stood a hoe.

She took up the hoehandle as she stepped on what a cursory glance had told her was a string of gaudy rag. It erupted to life, a copperhead flowing smooth as oil past her feet, across the worn floorboards, vanishing somewhere beneath them onto the blackgreen loam.

She screamed and whirled about with the hoe, running blindly for the door, for daylight, the hoehandle striking the back sides of the doorjamb, momentarily stopping her, and the wasps were instantly upon her. She dropped the hoe, stood in the doorway slapping wildly at her face.

She was still screaming. They were in her hair, down the neck of her blouse, she could feel them crawling over her breasts, stinging her face. She ran blindly into the yard.

She could hear running footsteps. He grabbed her, slapping at the wasps. Goddamn it to hell, he said. He grasped her skull roughly with both hands hard, moving them over her hair, she could feel his hands crushing the wasps on her scalp. He jerked her blouse off, beat at her breasts and shoulders, caught her in his arms, turned her wildeyed face up momentarily toward his own.

Where'd they sting you?

All over, she said, crying brokenly. My face, my breasts. Is that all of them?

I think so.

Then get the hell in the house.

She washed with cold water and coated her face with calamine lotion. She had taken most of the stings on her face and she could already feel it swelling. Her eyes seemed to be disappearing, her vision diminishing as if she peered through slits, knifeholes stabbed in the bloated flesh of her face.

Where were you?

Where was I? I was typing. Where did you think I was?

You could have come when I screamed. A damned copperhead practically ran over my foot and you were typing. I could have been bitten. I could be dead by now, and you would be typing.

I came when I heard you.

Sure. When you finished the paragraph. Or the page.

Goddamn it, Corrie, I came when I heard you. How did I know where you were? You know better than to be in that hot toolshed. What were you doing in there anyway? I thought you were on the porch.

You're never around when I need you. She began to cry.

You know that's not fair, Corrie.

It's the truth. I don't give a damn anymore what's fair and what's not.

She lay in the darkness, her eyes swathed in artificial darkness of cold wet bandages, listening to him typing. She wondered what time it was, if he would cook her supper or insist on her doing it. Or more likely, just do without.

After a while the typing ceased. The door opened.

Corrie, you want some tomato soup?

No.

What do you want?

Nothing. I want to be let alone. I don't want you looking at me.

Before her eyes swelled closed, she had looked with horror at herself: a bloated nightmare in the bathroom mirror, tiny dark eyes like bits of coal sinking in the softwhite suet of her face, tiny nose and curious kewpie mouth stuck onto an enormous balloon being inflated as she watched.

You want to go to the doctor?

I don't know. Do you think it could hurt the baby?

No.

After a while he went out. The door closed. The typing resumed. She lay listening to the whir of the air conditioner.

When she awoke, her eyes were not as swollen. She could see a little. Night had fallen beyond the window.

She wasn't sure what woke her until she heard it again. A knock on the other side of the wall.

David?

No answer. She waited. It came again, a hard preemptory knock such as something hard striking the paneled wall. A knock again, a sound of something falling against the wall and slithering down it.

Oh, Jesus. A walking stick, she thought, sick at heart, thinking about her father. She got up, opened the door. David? she called. The typing had ceased. It must be late. David? She went through the foyer, her vision still impaired, everything dark and blurry. She went onto the porch. Cool night air on her hot swollen face—she could smell cigarette smoke, hear the creek running.

David?

What is it? He was sitting on the porch steps, his head leant against a column. Staring off toward the toolshed.

What are you doing?

Resting. What are you doing?

There was something beating on the walls.

He didn't say anything.

I thought it might be you.

No, he said. It wasn't me.

It was beating on the bedroom wall.

It was?

What are you doing?

Thinking about those wasps. We'll have to get some spray and a sprayer and wipe them out. I don't know what to do about the snake. I don't relish ripping up that old floor.

Just stick a match to the whole thing. That's what I'm going to do.

No, he said gently. We can't do that. But I'll kill the snake, Corrie, I promise you.

Somebody's going to get bitten if you don't.

I said I would.

When are you coming to bed?

Not now. I just need to unwind. In a few minutes.

I wish you would. I'm afraid in there.

I will in a minute.

She went back inside. Her head ached, and when she lay back down the bed seemed to turn drunkenly, to tilt, so instinctively she clutched the covers. She wondered if there was any way the baby could have been affected.

She thought about her father. For a moment his face was frozen in her mind with the clarity of a photograph. His image would not recede: the pale almost protuberant eyes, the bony ridge across his forehead, the pale scalp through the receding reddishgray hair.

They had been living in Chicago when Ruthie called. They had flown to Knoxville that same night to find the old man seemingly better; Ruthie, prone to exaggeration, had him near death of a heart attack, the flowers already ordered likely as not, but the old man himself said he was tough as the butt cut of a whiteoak log.

Ruthie and Vern flew back to Florida. Vern ran a hotel there, and it wasn't often he could get away. Corrie said, well, as long as they were there they'd stay a few days with her father. Her father had never really liked David, and she was thinking that a few days might bring them, if not closer, at least to some understanding of each other. Her father was a merchant, and David was so far outside the normal range of his realm of acquaintances they might have been from different planets.

They had been making love for what must have been hours that night when the first knock came on the wall, David thrusting deep inside her, nearing orgasm, continuing despite the knocks and her attempt to get up, his arms tightening about her, his weight pinning her to the bed.

I have to see about him.

In a minute.

It may be time for his heart medicine.

He did not reply nor alter the rhythm of his thrusting. She was suddenly devoid of sensation, pushing at him, not playing anymore. The knock came again, and she was fighting him, trying to unwrap his arms, to stop the metronomic piston stroke inside her. She felt cold there between her legs, dead. His arms felt strong as steel bands, his stomach slapping hers. She could feel his hot breath on her throat.

She heard him fall against the wall, slide down it. David, please, she was crying, feeling him thrusting faster, beginning to come just as she shoved with all her might against him, forcing him off the side of the bed onto the floor, his penis sliding out of her.

Goddamn, David said.

She had a momentary vision of him leaping up, standing there naked and outraged, pendulous cock swinging. For a long time, that was the way she saw him: an enormous engorged penis swinging from a diminutive insignificant little man so far behind it you could barely make him out.

Her father was dead when she ran into the room, his face slack, eyes bulging and dull.

The will was read. There was twelve thousand dollars. Corrie had been his favorite.

Yet no one knew about that knock except she and David, and they had never spoken of it. The closest to an apology he had come was the gentle way he treated her the next week or so.

No one knew, so she must have dreamed it. Or, she had half a thought she wouldn't let herself pursue: the house knew.

Late in the afternoon he would walk back across the fields and watch dark fall over the homeplace. Dusk gathered first in the dell where lay the ruins of the old houseplace, and it seemed to Binder that dusk dwelt there always, crept out when the shadows lengthened like ink seeping into blotting paper. He knelt against a great beech and smoked his third cigarette of the day, watched the mosaic of trees go dimensionless and depthless, jagged brushstrokes rendering black trees against the paler heavens. A solitary whippoorwill called. Night birds took up the cry. A moon of palest rose cradled up out of the hollow, cypresses darkened to red as the day waned. Dusk drew on and the moon turned the color of blood, fierce and malign, enormous, he felt he could rise and stretch his arms and touch it. A foreign moon out of another age and another world, it should have risen over Stonehenge a thousand years ago. The skeletal pear tree turned to a twisted hieroglyphic of blackened bone, a clue left him by a prior race could he but decipher it.

David, he could hear her calling, and for a moment he had forgotten who and where he was and the voice seemed to have drifted across a hundred years of ruined landscape.

He crushed the cigarette carefully against the heel of his shoe and arose. He went through the old cemetery, mostly given now to scrub sassafras and sumac, marble tombs, graven angels and crumbling spires recumbent in poison oak rising out of the honeysuckle. The lettering so worn you could hardly tell the tale. Old musty yellowed yesterdays, a bloody deranged tale carried to the grave. He thought of the bones beneath this quiet hillside, of the secrets he would never know, the words he would never hear, that had never even been spoken, and he felt an almost tangible sense of loss. JACOB BEALE, the oblong block of granite read, NOW AT REST. Somehow Binder doubted it.

He loved the solitude, the dreamy sameness of the days. Time folded in on itself, one century the same as the next. Time was really only a concept, he thought, a way to get a handle on things, and he had discovered that he didn't need it: the house must have looked the same a hundred years ago. And the same dark enigma dwelt here then.

He didn't watch TV anymore except videocassettes with Stephie. He particularly didn't watch the news anymore. It had come to seem absurd, the curious doings of folk he wanted no truck with, folks fighting and dying in obscure countries for no reason he could fathom, Mercedes-driving good-old-boy evangelists with the clayest of feet, caught in seedy motel rooms playing doctor with whores.

It wasn't real, none of them were and he wanted no part of any of it. The IRS wasn't real, nor the CIA or the FBI or IRA or IBM or NBC. It was a game, a complex invention of boys playing grownup, a way to while away the time until the dark fell.

What was real was the slow timeless heart of midday, the sleepy drone of insects, the almost imperceptible murmur of the creek, and the hypnotic way the greengold pillars of light fell shifting through the trees into the haunted dell. The endless-looking fields that undulated away toward vague blue-looking woods, fireflies bobbing random as spirit lights. These are things that matter, he thought, and wondered about the wasted years when he hadn't known, with a kind of resigned regret. These are things with an aura of permanence about them.

That and the intangible mystery he could not put his finger on, which changed and teased like a will-o'-the-wisp, achingly nostalgic, faintly erotic, a musky heady taste in the back of his mouth, like a lost fragment of a dream or a life he ought to be able to retrieve could he just put his mind to it.

At some clockless hour he arose stiffly from the typewriter and placed what finished manuscript he had in a manila envelope and fastened the thumbclasp and stored it in a desk drawer. Corrie had always read his work and let him know in subtle ways if she thought he was getting a little flamboyant but he was going to sit on this. He wasn't sure if it was good or bad or indifferent but he did know it was the stuff of nightmares.

He also knew it would be useless to try sleeping for another two or three hours: he slept now when the house slept, as if in some curious way their cycles had become synchronous, catching catnaps in the daytime, dozing in the hot still honeysuckle afternoons. He knew the house was awake now, he could stand in its center and feel its heart beating around him, synced with his own breathing when he breathed, feel its attention on him, alert and focused as a cat watching a broken-winged bird.

He went out. The night was hot and still, holding its breath, not a leaf in motion. The creek murmurous across the polished stone. A whippoorwill called from some vague hollow far away and lost in the dark.

The toolshed was burnished silver in the moonlight, the rusted roof draining off what light there was, the canted door showing a wedged-shaped section of darkness. It was like no darkness that ever was, at once forbidding and achingly evocative and utterly foreign. His feet were damp with dew soaking through his sneakers before he even knew he was approaching it.

He went in the door, the rusted hinge protesting, a darkness here moonlight would not defray. At first he could see nothing, stood swaying in the hot still dark like a man unbalanced by wind or coalesced out of the darkness as if he were consciously creating them, and coincident with his dim vision felt the heat just leave, suddenly just not there anymore, trickles of perspiration down his ribcage gone icecold, the still fetid air, the cold charnel smell of the grave, and the hair prickled on his forearms and at the back of his neck.

There was a manlike bulk crouched in the corner of the toolshed. Heavyset hunkered the way a country man might sit, whittling, and very still, just something manlike and undistinguished moving the old singletrees and tracechains, smell that seemed to take him down bowered dusty roads to a long time ago, a smell compounded of sweat and tobacco and the smell of the warm earth and horses and the springtime smell of time itself, distillate and aphrodisiac.

Then the dark bulk stirred and a slurred voice said out of the darkness: Get you a little drink good buddy.

In a space between the boxing over the door lintel of the toolshed he found a half pint of whiskey three-quarters full: somebody's hidey-hole, he guessed. He had long become obsessive about searching for artifacts of the place's past, old bottles, broken tools, nameless chunks of rusted metal, an old one-bitted ax head he found beneath the rotted floorboards. Anything with threads of the past stringing off it, if you didn't know what the lock looked like, who knew what the key might be?

He unscrewed the cap and drank. Sweet Jesus that's awful, he said, and a low chuckle came from the corner of the toolshed. In the oblique moonlight he was someone else and he was somewhere he had never been before. He slid the bottle backhanded into a hippocket he hadn't known he had and the dried-out brogan workshoes he was wearing chafed his ankles. He was walking through luxuriant thick wild oats that came up to his thighs, the path trending through them gleamed like quicksilver, vanished. The world was the same yet different.

The house still sat on its knoll against the hillside but there was no light now, nothing but the brooding bulk of wood and stone and the moonlight on the windows and even the trees looked different, lusher, more opulent, and when he turned, there was a cornfield where no cornfield should be, the rows clocking away into nothingness, the stalks blueblack and gleaming.

A dog brushed the calf of his leg and wended away, toward the creek, without noticing him. Somewhere along the creekbank lost to him in the shadows beneath the sycamores came a young girl's laughter, achingly sweet and pure and nostalgic as the tinkling sound of some long-lost childhood carnival carillon. He was seized with longing so intense it ached in his chest, he wanted it always to keep, to drag out secretly and study it like a yellowed photograph, and he thought I am home, this is me, this is where I have been rambling down to all these years.

The moon rode above him, cold and still as a world locked in ice. When he raised his head to study it, it was no moon he knew, a moon of other seasons comfortless and uncaring and utterly remote.

A part of him stood aside and thought this is a dream, but I have got to remember this, there is something here I can use. Some lines from W. H. Auden drifted through his mind.

> The stars are not wanted now: put out every one:
> Pack up the moon and dismantle the sun;
> Pour away the ocean and sweep up the wood.
> For nothing now can ever come to any good.

The creaking of the toolshed hinges drew him slowly around; his body felt foreign to him, awkward, an older man's body, ill-used and heavy. The canted door swung slowly outward on its one good hinge, and a tide of black blood erupted soundlessly onto the silver grass. The blood pooled in the lowbank near the creek, rising incrementally, foaming in the thick wild oats, eddying onto the worn footpath, staining the moonwhitened road that wound to the bridge. He could feel it lapping about his ankles.

Then in an eyesblink it was gone and he could smell the dew and the wild oats again and three men were clambering over the wooden gate and dropping into the barn lot, dusting themselves off and crossing the yard toward the house, an old frockcoated man with muttonchop whiskers and a heavyset prosperous-looking man in a broad-brimmed hat and a felt-hatted black who walked with a stifflegged shambling gait. They seemed to be talking animatedly among themselves although he could hear no sound. One by one they vanished, as if they filed off the edge of the earth. Then a voice in Binder's ear said, almost conversationally, Slit the little roundheeled whore's throat, is what I'd do. A voice sourceless and genderless and somehow mechanical and Binder didn't even wonder if it was talking to him or not.

A weight of morning light on his eyelids, featureless yellow world, reality seeping in, he awoke by degrees, like a drunk remembering the places he was and the things he did. The toolshed, he thought. Jesus Christ, what's the matter with me. He felt strange and dislocated, half afraid to open his eyes, caught in the strand of the dream he half wanted to hang onto. Come on, he said, you're a tough guy. You can do it. He became aware of white ceilings, walls of deep rose, the comforting whir of the air conditioner. He remembered Corrie saying: You had too much to drink last night, and another part of his mind said, Hell yes, the electric pruner, that's what the damn manlike bulk was.

Corrie slept beside him, her dark hair tousled, a careless arm thrown across her face, and a wave of love and gratitude hit him with such force it left him dizzy. Then he saw the butcher knife. It had been inserted between Corrie's pillow and the mattress, perhaps eight or ten inches. Beyond her tanned face he could see an inch or so of serrated blade and the fingergrip rosewood handle.

He got up incrementally careful not to jar the bed, noticing without surprise that he was naked, his bare feet clotted with wild oat seeds, soundless across the carpet. She stirred as he eased the knife from beneath the pillow, her eyes opened beneath his face, startled and blue, so close. Lefthanded he slid the knife out of sight under the bed, stroked her cheek with his right. Her eyes were depthless and guileless, so close to his own, eyes you could drown in. Abruptly tears stung his eyes and he hid his face in the soft hollow of her throat. Why, baby, she said, and raised a tender hand to stroke his hair.

It could work the TV now. Stephie had seen it do it with Pooh and Piglet twice. But intuitively she knew that it did not work the electronic things inside the back of the TV but with the things inside her mind or her head. Daddy said the brain was electronic too, just a very complex computer that ran on tiny bits of electricity, but she didn't believe it and Mommy didn't either. Mommy said God made it and no man could make anything approaching the mind because the mind was sacred. It had a soul, you unplug it and all it was was a bunch of junk.

She had watched Pooh four or five times before and already knew it word for word, scene for scene. It was the one about the blustery day, when it was raining all over the Hundred Acre Wood.

Daddy was taking a break from writing, and she was sitting on his lap in the recliner, the chair tilted back and Daddy's socked feet bookending each side of the TV set, Mommy on the couch hemming a pair of curtains, a homey scene out of *Leave It to Beaver*.

The soundtrack was singing, The rain, rain, rain came down, down, down. Pooh and Piglet and Tigger were rambling through the Hundred Acre Wood looking for a house for Owl, Tigger bounding on ahead. They came through a spinney of larch onto a stony field stumbling downhill in the sun, and at the bottom of the field stood the old toolshed, angular and oblique, in the midday heat, the sides encroached with poison oak, greenblack, and simultaneously with the sight of the toolshed Daddy jumped and she could feel the harsh intake of his breath in her hair. The image flickered, muted, as if some light tremor had jarred the Hundred Acre Wood, rumbled way beneath the earth. Daddy had relaxed against the cushions and she knew intuitively that he wasn't seeing what she was anymore.

Mommy was watching the set blandly, a half smile on her face, and Stephie knew that she hadn't seen anything at all except Milne's cartoon world.

Pooh and Piglet and Tigger were clustered before the canted cedar door, gesturing and talking. Piglet seemed to be trying to convince them to go inside the toolshed, Pooh hanging back, he looked confused and frightened, Piglet tugging at his arm, impatient, at length dragging him into the darkness.

Stephie leant forward, straining to see, Daddy said something murmurously and interrogatory, she couldn't tell what. They were in now. She had seen with detached amazement that it was the same toolshed, the rotted floorboards rendered in Disney animation, the motley of tools strewn about the cartoon walls. Piglet had taken up an ax.

Something sinister here, the soundtrack had altered, there was a hypnotic buzz in her ears. Above it Daddy said, What the hell, not in shock or disbelief. She was feeling a mild hint of irritation, as if the picture was messed up.

Mommy looked up. What is it, David? she asked, precisely as Beaver Cleaver's mother might have said it. David mumbled something she couldn't hear.

What?

Hell of a thing to put in a cartoon for kids, he said, and looking up, Stephie saw that he looked confused, as if he was himself not quite certain what he had seen. She turned back to the TV.

I think you left your mind in gear and it rolled away, Corrie said.

Piglet drove the ax into Pooh's forehead, rocked it back and forth to dislodge it from the bone that anchored it, swung it savagely again and Pooh went down, his face pumping blood, not cotton or Styrofoam or other synthetic fiber, but a thick gout of foaming scarlet, Pooh trying to crawl toward the door and the ax falling metronomically, bisecting a cartoon rendering of flesh and muscle and splintered bone, Tigger making a mad scramble toward the door that the ax suddenly blocked, and before she knew what happened, she was vomiting, her stomach recoiling and spewing out a steaming barrage of hot acidic liquid onto David's lap, David clutching her up, saying, Jesus, what's the matter, Stephie simultaneously vomiting and crying, at last choking out, Turn it off, to Corrie who had jumped up startled, the curtains fallen and forgotten.

Later, she was sick off and on all night, Corrie up with her, up and down to the bathroom. Coming through the living room sometime in the small hours of the morning, Stephie was startled to find the TV on, David stretched out on the couch watching it.

Jesus, David. Pooh at three o'clock in the morning? Corrie said disgustedly.

Daddy, Stephie said, and when he didn't reply she thought he was asleep: but when she approached him she saw he wasn't, his eyes were open but did not seem to remark her, instead watched with a kind of bemused confusion the frolicking of cartoon animals on the particolored screen.

———

At night there were dreams of old plagues that the morning would not quite erase. From the first, the house just did not feel right to Corrie. It just did not feel right, like any house where a family would live and raise children. She could not quite put her finger on the word she wanted, and suddenly the word unclean drifted into her mind. That's what it is, she thought, the place is filthy: though not in a literal sense, for the people Greaves hired had certainly done an adequate job. The place was spotless, as spotless as you would expect a hundred-year-old house to be. The trim was newly painted, the hardwood floors stripped and sanded and revarnished, the brightly colored drapes she had chosen should have brought life and freshness into the rooms, but they did not. The house seemed to absorb everything into itself, to darken everything a shade, to suck the very life out of it and leave a dry husk.

For no reason she could discover, the house made her think of the grandfather who had died when she was a child. Diseased, she thought, that is precisely the word I meant. There is something very wrong with the house, it has a cancerous growth in the insides that keeps ticking away like a time bomb. There seemed to be a dark malignancy in the bowels of the house. And after this, she became aware of its smell. Beneath the smell of paint and varnish and the crisp smell of new fabric, there was an undercurrent of malevolence, a smell no amount of cleaning would erase, the persistent seeping yellowbrown odor of the sickroom where someone is dying a slow death from cancer.

Diseased. And the house, something in the light or lack of it, played tricks on you. It caught you when you weren't paying attention and brought you back. You thought you saw things out of the corners of your eyes. She didn't believe in ghosts, thought the whole thing absurd, but there was no way around admitting that once she thought she glimpsed a woman in a green dress pass the window. She turned and it was gone. The ground floor of the house was flanked by a covered porch on the front and both sides and that was another thing she hated, the way the house looked and the sickening smell of flowers, not living flowers but the drying withering smell of banked funeral flowers. The ground-floor porches were too wide and they gave the house a disproportionate aspect, absurdly like a humped old woman with full skirts. The woman had been walking up the west side of the porch toward the front of the house, but of course there had been no one there and Stephie was playing quietly in the front yard and she felt like a fool for looking.

It just became one of the things she didn't think about much lately, the things she filed away to be looked into later. Like the way David was absorbed in what he was writing, so much more so than with the first book. He didn't even want to go into town anymore and put it off as long as possible. And the way Stephie did little except sit in front of the TV or reread books she had read dozens of times. Every day was waiting, every day was like life lived in airline terminals, bus stations, the waiting rooms of expensive specialists in terminal diseases.

But mostly the way one day segued into the next, each the deadly same, the hot sun baking everything, the white dusty road empty as a broken promise, not even a Bible salesman or a lost tourist to break the monotony. Days came and they went and she forced the inevitable frustration out of her mind, almost physically pushing them away, thinking, It's only for the summer, one summer out of all the summers of our lives, it seemed a minimal price to pay: for she knew the book was working. She had read the letter from David's agent, but she had known already. If the book worked the way David wanted and everybody believed in it and promoted it and it was a bestseller, she could quit worrying about the money. The money and Stephie's school and all this morbid, sickening bullshit about ax murderers and hundred-year-old poltergeists and just get on with it, with their lives, go somewhere bright and cheerful, Florida maybe, swim in the sun and the salty sea with the diseased smell completely out of her nostrils, this monstrous, diseased homeplace no more than a bad memory, a day gone with no more to show than a number on the calendar, what I did on my summer vacation.

The snakes, the wasps, and then the sounds through the wall were all Corrie could stand, especially when she thought of Stephie. They agreed to let Stephie go stay with friends of the family for a few weeks, until school started or they moved back to Chicago for the winter.

The weather that year turned unseasonal. In late July the temperature climbed into the nineties and stayed there except occasionally when it eased over the one-hundred-degree mark. It was a fierce and strange malign heat that became a tangible presence, bad company that will not go home. The earth grew dry and fissured, miniature cataclysms appeared in the parched clay, widened and deepened, creeping like bower vines across the blistered dry earth.

Some days dawned with the mocking promise of rain but the sun hanging over the eastern field withdrew it, the dew vanishing, the bog along the lowland almost instantly sucked into nothingness until all there was was a malevolent red sun tracking across the horizon into a sky gone marvelously blue and absolutely cloudless.

Old men at their checker games allowed it had not been so dry and hot since the thirties, they could not agree on precisely what year. The secondary roads turned to a shifting layer of dust that rose listlessly in the slipstreams of passing automobiles, drifting down, talcuming the greenblack honeysuckle shrouding the shoulders of the road. Farmers began to fear for their crops, stood out at night studying the skies for a sign that was not there. Corn began to yellow in the field, the blades twisting limply on themselves in defeat. At night heat lightning flickered in the far-off dark, vague and impotent.

After unrelenting days of this, tempers grew short and there were random outbursts of violence. People did things they ordinarily would not have done, began to think the old laws did not apply. Calvin Huggins, a local pinball cowboy, would-be poolshark, the kind of gambler who raises his draw to an inside straight, was the first to make a fatal mistake. He drank a cold beer on payday when the shoe factory let off. He was sitting on a stool in the Snow White Café, the end one nearest the air conditioner, feeling the pleasant warmth from his paycheck through his pocket and cold beaded beer bottle against his palm and he thought of his wife home in the hot little rental house with the busted air conditioner, probably waiting on the money and he for no good reason other than the fact that this was payday and he was red and worn out from the heat suddenly thought, To hell with her. Her face, bitter and accusatory, drifted freefall into his mind. Fuck her, he thought. I never could do anything to suit her anyhow. He bought a roll of quarters for the pinball machine. The pinball machine had been at the back of his mind all day anyway, like a glamour woman who probably won't but just possibly will. He went home at midnight drunk and broke, the grocery money and rent fed quarter by quarter down the remorseless gullet of the pinball machine.

At noon the next day, he was under the Pontiac Firebird that was his pride and joy, a metallic brown, just the color of the one Rockford had driven on TV, replacing the brake pads. He was on the last one, the right front, and had been moving the bumper jack corner to corner. He was ever one to tempt fate, it is a fact that a man who will draw to an inside straight will trust a bumper jack.

She watched from the porch with eyes that were just smoldering hate in her face.

Hey, you bringing that beer like I said or do I have to rattle your head around a little more?

Wordlessly, she brought the can of beer.

Set it on that block and hand me them fuckin visegrips, his final words.

The jack was tilted ever so slightly. Perhaps a finger might dislodge it, the weight of a cool evening breeze. Her eyes found there was a crowbar leant against a cottonwood and without even thinking, she took it up and positioned her feet and slammed the crowbar against the post of the jack with all her might. The jack skewed crazily, went sidewise and the drum came down on his right temple as he reached backhanded for the beer. She went in the house and stood at the sink washing dishes thinking no thoughts at all and watching nothing whatsoever out the window, and when she was sure he was dead she dialed 911 to tell them about the accident.

Long a watcher of the changes of the seasons and a believer in signs and portents, Annie Mae Hicks came out of a network of clay gullies just at dusk dragging an armful of honeysuckle vines and saw the first light bobbing across the field, angling down a distant rise toward the homeplace, a yellow light, not blinking as a firefly does but erratic as a lantern slung along by a man's side. She didn't think whose or what side it might be: she didn't want to know. She just thought, so it's finally back, but there was a kind of detachment, then a giddy relief. She knew intuitively it had nothing to do with her. Not this time. It's them, she thought, them Yankees or whoever: I got nothing it wants anymore.

Her husband told it around town about the lights but no one paid much attention to him, he had cried wolf once too often. No one believed him exactly but still there was something about the Beale farm.

Coy Hickerson put it into words in the shade of the magnolia in the courthouse yard, trying to distract his partner into not noticing the potentially fatal move he had made on the checkerboard. Sometimes I think it'd be a good thing if that place burnt to the foundation.

You can't burn dirt, Cagle said.

I don't believe none of that bullshit about lights and voices, but I do believe in luck and that place is just as unlucky as it gets. Nobody never had any dealings at all with that place that didn't come to a bad end. Them Beales had the right idea, just get the hell away from it and let somebody else sweat out the hard times.

Them Abernathy sisters lived out there till a few years ago, a man said from the circle of watchers. Nothing ever happened to them.

Hell, they died, Charles Cagle said, seeing the move and taking his double jump. Anyway, times don't get no harder than that.

Everybody dies, that's a given. They's different ways of doing it.

Ginseng digging on the northeast corner of the Beale land, Thurl Cogdill slipped off a steep limestone bluff and broke his neck against a beech tree forty feet below and the searchers didn't find him for a week. There was no way a truck could get in and out of there and they had to carry him, hot heavy work when you're holding your breath, zigzagging the bluff, and lash him to the back of a four-wheeler ATV. Thurl was known to be addicted to 'sang digging and they figured he had seen a bunch he just couldn't resist. They were partly right. He had seen a four-prong bunch and a little patch of threes on a ledge against the cliff wall and he hesitated only momentarily before climbing out after it.

It was no big thing and he had been in more perilous places without mishap but something drew his eyes up from the hole he was scratching in the flinty soil and there was a black Mastiff coming around the ledge, not walking or running, just coming, gliding as implacable as a locomotive, something from a bad dream. The sight of the enormous black dog was disturbing enough. When the ledge curled around an outcropping of limestone the dog came straight through the fissured blue rock and for a fraction of a second it was translucent, the opaque of the rock filtered through the head and shoulders of the dog. Not remarking him, looking like a dog but acting like no dog Thurl had ever seen, he saw too late the dog was making no attempt to avoid him: it was just coming on. He scrambled upright just as the dog passed through the calf of his right leg, the leg going suddenly numb and cold, brittle as ice. Thurl panicked and half-mad with unreasoning fear and just wanting gone, away from the dog at whatever cost, overbalancing backward and windmilling his arms madly as if he might at this late date learn flight.

The woods turned sere and dry and volatile as gunpowder. Forest fires sprang up, random as the deaths by outbreaks of violence. The air carried the nostalgic scent of woodsmoke and at sunset the air was tinted a hazy blue like Indian summer. The fire was creeping down from Shipps Bend and at night you could watch it feed, the distant line of fire pulsing fine and bright as a burning thread.

Binder climbed out of the bed of the pickup truck with the other three men and turned to help unload the rakes and shovels. The smell of smoke was very strong. He could see it shifting in the air far down the slope and out in what appeared to be a clearing of some sort. He could see the fire approaching, an orange glow that suddenly intensified both in brightness and in speed, enormous showers of sparks shooting upward and the field seemed abruptly to explode.

Boys, that's reached the sage field, one of the men called, and coming like a goddamned freight train.

Their faces were alternately light and shadow, the strobic orange fire, the moving shadows of the lowering trees.

Binder felt suddenly out of place, wondered why he had bothered to come. The only reason he was there at all was because he had seen a load of firefighters disembarking a flatbed truck in town, and the men had looked so bonetired and weary that the radio announcements beseeching volunteers he had been hearing suddenly became real to him. Their pale eyes burned out of faces and they looked timeless, no part of the eighties, old sepia daguerreotypes, men out of the dustbowl thirties.

Though if he admitted it, the whole truck was a little more complex than that. He had sat on the front porch and watched the smoke, the smoke that rose as if from distant battlefields, and there was a panicky feeling at the back of his mind that the battles were getting closer and he had to choose up sides, that fire might do to the Beale farm what a hundred years of time had not been able to do.

What are we supposed to be doing? he asked.

Hell, we got a gravy train here, the man nearest him said. You lucked out. The state's already plowed a firebreak and all we got to do is wait.

The men were smokeblacked and weary. They smelled of trees, earth, smoke, and sweat. They had come from the fire at Shipps Bend, Binder and the rest of the volunteers being split up and sent with experienced crew who had already been fighting the fires.

He looked around for someone he might recognize and was surprised to see Charlie Cagle leaning against a tree watching the fire.

Mr. Cagle, he said, I see they got you out here.

Ain't it hell? Cagle said. They're down to seeds and stems. Nothin left but little boys and old men like me.

The men formed a loose circle around Binder and Cagle, some leaning on shovels, others hunkered against the boles of trees watching the fire cross the field.

Didn't figure to see you here. Don't reckon they get many forest fires in Chicago.

I'm really from East Tennessee, I was only in Chicago for a few months. Woods burn up in the mountains, too.

You the feller lives out on the old Beale place? another asked.

That's me.

Then it don't surprise me, you bein here. I know I'd rather fight fire in the piney woods than go to bed ever night out where you do.

Why's that?

Don't pay him no mind, Binder, the first man said. Clyde's a notorious chickenshit. He's known for it across five or six counties around here.

Not too chickenshit to kick your sorry ass, Clyde said. Too damn tired maybe.

There was an easy camaraderie among the men that Binder had occasionally aspired to but never attained, no matter how hard he tried it always seemed the seams of his effort always showed force, and there was a distance between himself and others he could not breach.

Hell we might as well set, Cagle said, hunkering down and rubbing his knees. Nothin to do till it gets to the firebreak.

What if it crosses? Binder asked.

It won't if the wind don't get up, Cagle told him. The break ought to be wide enough to hold it but they got us strung out here to beat out what little fires spring up from burnin leaves blowed across. It don't take but a minute for a little bitty fire to be a great big one.

I seen you around town but I never met you, a man said out of the dark. He stuck out a grimy hand and Binder shook it. My name's Buster Sharp, and we was just joshing you about where you live. That place has just always had a bad reputation. Anybody willing to pick up a shovel and help, I ain't about to piss him off. I expect you've heard plenty about that place from folks you've met.

Actually I haven't met hardly anybody, Binder said. Mr. Cagle and Frazier, the A/C man. The only other person I met I never learned who he was. He just beat the hell out of me right quick and left.

Say he did? Where at, in town?

No, out on the farm. I walked up on him in the woods there back of the old Beale house, told him who I was and stuck my hand out the way you just did. He hit me a time or two before I knew what was going on and when I got up he was gone into the woods. Binder laughed. He was real too, there wasn't anything ghostly about him. My jaw was sore for a week.

Didn't he say anything?

He said something about snaketraps. I didn't get all of it.

Son of a bitch, Sharp said, Aaron Swaw.

That's Swaw all right. His mama was the only one of Owen's kids that survived. He traps snakes with rabbits in cages. Big heavyset fella with one eye cocked off toward Memphis or somewheres.

Well he was big. It was about dusk when I met him and I didn't get a real good look at him.

———

Swaw was a nightmare waiting for a dreamer, lying sweating on his cot in the humid dark going through the list he carried in his head. The list was the name of folks who had done him grievances, real or imagined. A sense of the power he possessed made him giddy and almost ecstatic there in the darkness. With a match to be had for the asking he could destroy anyone he wanted to, and when blame was handed out no one would even think of him.

There was a farmer named Milford on Jacks Branch who had run him off twice for hunting: the second time he had even gotten the drop on Aaron with a .30-06 and taken the brace of squirrels. He had called Aaron names Aaron was not accustomed to answering to. Had he known that his own name had been mentally entered on a little white card in Aaron's head and that he was just waiting for his lottery number to come up, his sleep would have been more troubled than it was.

As it was he got off light. Aaron only burned his barn. He watched from the hilltop above the farm by the orange flicker. He could see miniature black figures darting about the barn lot, impotent and spastic as the jerking of marionettes on strings. Aaron lay in the leaves and had no word for what he felt, it was better than anything, better than the whitebreasted woman on the Beale farm.

The next night he lay and thought of David Binder, though what he saw in his mind was not a name but a face. He did not even know his name, just thought of him as the Yankee. But he was saving Binder: Binder he was intending to kill, wanted to kill, there was something crazy in his eyes. Binder was going to burn in his sleep and all his family was going to burn with him but he had plans for the woman first, all that he was wanting was the opportunity, and it would come round, it always had before.

Labor Day Weekend, 1982

Vern was a lover, Binder thought, surely amused, watching him study himself critically in the hall mirror. Vern fancies himself a ladies' man. Vern was leant to the glass, peering closely at his face in the poor light. Now comb your hair, Binder said to himself. Vern took a pocket comb from his hippocket and ran it through his hair, eyed the result. His hair was the color of bright copper wire and it was naturally curly. Binder knew it was naturally curly. Vern had told him.

Even if he had not seen Vern scrutinizing himself in the mirror, Binder would have known Vern considered himself a ladies' man. It was inherent in the clothes he wore, a kind of pseudowestern rigging boots and a yokebacked cowboy shirt, jeans riding low on his hips. It was encoded in his very stance, a kind of urban dream of a cowboy's lockhipped work. The very essence of macho, Binder thought. He is a truck driver without a truck, a cowboy squinting in a carbon monoxide sunset.

There was other evidence as well. Sitting on the porch before supper, Vern had told him while Corrie and her sister Ruthie were in the kitchen.

You talk about women, Vern said. Boy, you know a motel operator meets a world of women.

Is that a fact, Binder said noncommittally.

Vern lowered his voice, glanced toward the screen door. It damn sure is. Them old gals on the run…dodgin their husbands, dodgin their boyfriends…calling me up at all hours to come down to their rooms, this ain't right, that ain't right. Givin me them up-and-down looks. That old long eye. Run in, run out, what's Ruthie to know? What's fifteen minutes?

Fifteen minutes is not very long, Binder said bemusedly, studying the wind in the sedge above the creek, the gradations of failing light. Binder could look at seemingly insignificant things for hours, losing himself in them. Now he was far away, lost in last week's work, before Vern and Ruthie came for the Labor Day holiday.

Vern considered Binder's reply for a time. What's that supposed to mean? Fifteen minutes is not very long.

It doesn't mean anything.

Vern was placated. He leaned closer, gouged Binder in the ribs with an elbow, winked. This old gal one time, he said, peering intently into Binder's face, said she was from Omaha. Rung me up on room service and I went down there and knocked on the door. Come in, she says. Son, she was spread out there on the bed buck naked. I mean not a stitch on. That thing gaped open like a alligator's mouth.

Binder didn't say anything.

Don't you believe me?

Sure, Binder said.

How come you keep backing up?

I'm not backing up.

Yes, you are.

You get right up in my face to talk, Vern. I can hear you very well. I never could stand anybody right up in my face. The territorial imperative, I guess.

The what?

I never did like anybody grabbing my arm, either, Binder said, disengaging the fingers from his bicep.

Vern studied him. Maybe you're a latent homosexual, he said.

And maybe you're full of shit, Binder said amiably.

But the main reason Binder knew what Vern was was he had seen him looking at Corrie. Corrie had on a pair of very tight faded jeans and Vern had been staring at her crotch, where the denim was pulled taut over the upthrust pelvic bone. Corrie had been looking away toward the creek, the sun in her face, animatedly talking to Ruthie, unaware of Vern's scrutiny. Like the true ladies' man he was, Vern didn't care who was looking. He was staring at her crotch with a kind of constrained hunger, momentarily forgetting where he was or that Ruthie and Binder might be watching. Binder remembered Vern's face with a kind of clinical detachment, as if he was watching the curious behavior of a stranger in a crowd. He told himself he had no feelings about it one way or another.

He just remembered it was all.

They played cards for a while. Binder and Vern were bored. Corrie and Ruthie weren't bored: they were sisters, and they didn't see each other very much. They had a lot to talk about, everything was a joke. It was a long way to Orlando, and Ruthie and Vern were always tied up at the motel.

Watching her study her cards, Binder thought how much Ruthie had changed. He remembered when he and Corrie married she had been an attractive girl, a little heavy on the baby fat, maybe, but with an aura of raw sexual awareness she made Binder immediately aware of. She'd treated him with a sort of big sisterly approach that seemed somehow tentative, subject to change at a moment's notice. Now she just projected an overblown blow-siness. There was a haphazard look to her and the dark roots of her blond hair were showing. Looking at Ruthie and Corrie together, Binder thought sardonically, Well, I got the pick of the litter all right.

Say, you got something to drink? Vern asked him.

I don't know. I think there's part of a bottle of Scotch around here somewhere. Do you know where it is, Corrie?

Somewhere in the cabinet. I remember putting it there.

What's the matter with you? You quit?

I seldom drink anymore.

He seldom drinks anymore. Ain't that pretty. Ain't that just like a writer. Writers seldom drink anymore. Anybody else would just say they quit.

He didn't say he quit, Vern, Ruthie said. He says he doesn't drink much. Quit picking on him.

You probably smoke that old dope, don't you?

No.

Ruthie turned to Binder. He's not happy unless he's picking at somebody. I don't know what's the matter with him. Picking is what he does best.

As if to remove all doubt of this, Vern continued. Will there be any women at this forsaken dance?

It's not a forsaken dance.

Vern was a few years older than Binder, and he seemed to have something to prove to him.

Will you please not be rude? Corrie had asked. I know you don't like Vern, but just try to get along for my sake.

All right, Binder had promised, and watching her face now across the card table he regretted it. He saw nothing left of the sweet gratuity that had been there, and he thought: she likes them.

She really does. Vern too. And he saw suddenly that they were no longer two couples. They had become three of a kind and a wild card.

While they slept, he went with his morning coffee toward the toolshed. The grass was lush and heavy with dew. Fog followed the line of the creek, crept ephemeral as smoke into the rank, weedy bottomland. Then the sun seemed to ascend visibly, the fog ascending with it coincident with a chorus of cicadas arising from the field and a crisp warm smell of summer dying. Already there was a remote look of distance to the heavens.

Night seemed to linger in the cloistered dark in the toolshed. He stood in the doorway for a moment, allowing his eyes to adjust to the diminished light. Objects formed out of formlessness, as if creating themselves: the dank earth floor, old oddments of metal, a motley of broken tools. A row of mason jars of cloudylooking foodstuffs. He could smell the dryly sour odor of years-old onions strung on the walls. Provender the optimistic old lady Abernathy had put by for a winter she didn't live to see.

It was there, lying in the fingers of sunlight that fell solid through the broken shakes. At first glance a once-gaudy scarf sun-aged to a faded iridescence, gleaming in the sun, burnished, metallic. He approached the board floor cautiously, hunkered on the dank earth watching the snake. Its head was toward him yet he moved with such stealthy caution it did not stir. Perhaps it dozed behind eternally open eyes, lulled by the timeless sanctity of the toolshed, or maybe it knew him by now.

He had come to kill it the first time he had seen it. A badly frightened and stillsobbing Corrie had decreed that it die, and he had stood leaning over it with an iron tamping bar in his hands, forty or fifty pounds of rusty metal that would have crushed its newpenny head to an unrecognizable wafer of mangled flesh. He held it paused a foot above the snake's head, feeling its weight, knowing that it would fall, but it did not.

He did not know exactly what had forestalled him. Certainly it did not look defenseless: a yard long and thicker than his wrist, with a lethal look of evil about it. It looked quite capable of taking care of itself. But maybe it's a female, he thought. Perhaps it has young. Who will suckle them? Why didn't Mommy come home, they would ask, though he did not believe it. There was nothing of the mother about her. The bar's weight heavier, his muscles knotted holding it, but still it would not fall, and he realized he was caught by eerie and evil beauty. Its skin looked coppery and bright, so iridescent there seemed to be depths to it, as if he could see through to the evil at its core, layered like the skin of an onion.

After the first time, he returned each morning. Most days it would be there in the sun. He guessed it made its home beneath the broken floor. He'd sip his coffee and watch it, smoke his first cigarette of the day lost in the complex pattern of its skin, finding there maps to places he'd never been, watching the play of the light on the scaled body as it moved.

Once he'd poked it with a long stick to see what it would do. It coiled instantly, exploding into a nearliquid smoothness of motion, all grace and purpose, head and stubby tail aloft, its mouth wide, fangs unhinged. It struck at the stick, waited. He waited, the stick motionless at length. He lowered it carefully. He sat still as death for a long time. At last the snake flowed over the boards and beneath the floor.

He knew there was something old and implacable and female about it—Little Sister Death, he named her, after a line from Faulkner, though he couldn't remember where he'd read it. It seemed to suit her.

David.

They were up. He could hear Corrie calling him in to breakfast. He drained the coffee cup, ground the cigarette butt out on the dank earth, and arose with painful slowness, backed out of the door into the bright September sun, as if he'd suddenly broken the surface of murky, polluted water.

Breakfast is ready.

All right, I'm coming, he said.

They had all been ready an hour awaiting Vern while he shaved and combed his hair just so and changed twice before he looked the way he wanted to look, and then nothing would do him but he must find a bootlegger.

That's the way Vern always is going out, Ruthie said. Men talk about women keeping them waiting, but I've never seen one take as much time with her hair and clothes as a man does.

David's not like that, Corrie said. He doesn't care how he looks.

Vern wants to look just right, Ruthie said, and there was a curious kind of pride in her voice, so that Binder thought, Ruthie knows Vern is a lover too.

Binder was driving. He didn't even want to go. He was feeling a little desperate, a seed of anger burning inside him, locked into this by the promise he'd made to Corrie. I don't know where to get a drink, he said. This is a dry county and I don't know any bootlegger. Wouldn't a beer do?

For a dance like this one? Hell, David, we can find us a bootlegger. Man can't go to a square dance without a little toddy in him.

A cab driver in Beale Station sold Vern four halfpints of peach brandy from the trunk of his cab, first making them drive down below the railroad tracks.

Binder drove back out Highway 20 and down Sinking Creek, Vern and Ruthie in the backseat taking turns at the bottle. Out the windshield, Binder watched the twisting country roads, the little unexpected rises rushing at you out of the night, the clearings where sat houses, the whiteframe homes of the country squires, the shotgun shacks of the disenfranchised.

Binder didn't know what he'd expected, but it wasn't what he found when they reached the dance. He guessed he'd been looking for old folks in Duckhead overalls, brighthaired girls in gingham dresses, an old toothless fiddler sawing out Appalachian reels, brogans clogging on scarred floors. Binder smiled wryly to himself. The enormous building looked like a converted rollerrink surrounded by four-wheel-drives. He couldn't hear any fiddles, either. There was music spilling out into the night, but it was hardedged rock and roll. The place was loud and alive; it had the air of a raucous country honkytonk.

Inside was more of the same: no alcohol was served but everyone seemed to be slipping into the night and returning drunk anyway, and once Binder caught the smell of marijuana smoke. No overalls. He even saw a pair of designer jeans, a few pairs of hundred-dollar cowboy boots. The trucks outside had deer rifles in the back windows, likely .357 Magnums in the gloveboxes. These good old boys had a curious air of militancy about them, and even the anthemistic song the band was playing bore this out: *I've got a shotgun a rifle and a four-wheel-drive and a country boy will survive.*

They all seemed to be having a good time. The floor was crowded with dancing couples, the air heavy and confusing with threads of conversation and laughter.

The four of them sat at a table near the bandstand, but only for a moment. Vern immediately grasped Ruthie's hand and they disappeared into the swirling dancers.

I wonder if they sell anything to drink here, he said to Corrie.

What?

He said it louder.

I don't know. Cokes, I guess. Why? Do you have a headache?

No, Binder said, but he did, the beginning of one. A bright, nagging flickering of pain like heat lightning behind his eyes.

She didn't believe him, he could tell, but she was solicitous. We'll move where it's less noisy when Vern and Ruthie get back.

The song ended and another began. Vern and Ruthie didn't return. Little by little Binder felt himself absorbing the cheerful ambience of the place. He began to feel a little better about things. He might even be able to write tonight, if Vern would leave him alone. He could feel the stirring of the desire to work that had lain dormant for the week Vern and Ruthie had been there, and when the band began a waltz he pulled a protesting Corrie from her chair and led her to the floor, her face blushed and pleased. She pillowed her face against his throat.

There he is, Binder told her. Vern's already promoting himself.

Vern in a crowd along the opposite wall was talking to a man in a cowboy hat. There was a young girl with long blond hair by the man's side. Vern seemed mainly to be talking to her. The man in the cowboy hat wasn't watching. The red slab of his face looked bored and distracted.

He's telling them how much he took in last year, Binder said. How close he is to Disney World, how full his motel is, how many miles his black Eldorado gets to the gallon. All those alligator mouths.

What?

Never mind. Something Vern told me to impress me.

Oh, just forget him, David. For a moment I thought you were actually having a good time.

When Ruthie returned to the table, Vern didn't. Ruthie had brought them all a tall paper cup of Coca-Cola and crushed ice. She looked about in mock caution, took a halfpint from her purse, then poured peach brandy into the Coke.

Vern just loves people, she said. He's a great mixer, I don't reckon he's ever seen a stranger in his life.

Yet her voice seemed to carry a diminished enthusiasm, as if she were growing more morose. Binder didn't see how you could get crying drunk on peach brandy and Coke, but she might. He guessed you might get sick, and that would be about as bad.

He's not a stick-in-the-mud like David is, she said, then smiled at him, as if to diminish the sting the words carried.

I like him just the way he is, Corrie said, her hand on David's arm.

They moved to a table near the door where it was quieter. After a while Vern glided up, seated himself between Ruthie and Corrie. He gestured toward the paper cups. Where's mine?

We figured your new friends would buy you one, Ruthie said. You seemed to have forgotten us.

There's a lot of nice folks here, he said, smiling broadly, winking lewdly at Binder, who didn't wink back.

David, who is that girl? Corrie asked.

Binder looked. A girl seemed to be watching him. She was standing in the open doorway, leaning on the jamb, framed against the summer night. A slim, tall blonde with flaxen hair, pale blue eyes. She was studying him intensely.

I don't know, he finally said.

Then why is she looking at you that way?

I don't know, Binder said again. Maybe she thinks she knows me.

Or maybe she does know you.

Oh for Christ's sake, Corrie. You know everybody in the county I do.

She was silent. What Binder had said was true, and Corrie knew it, yet she continued to watch the girl with a kind of annoyed perplexity.

Maybe she saw your picture on the jacket of your novel, Ruthie said.

I doubt it, Binder said lightly. I think it only sold two copies in Tennessee, and they were both sold in Blount County.

Mention of Binder's book, especially by Ruthie, did not set well with Vern. That looks like a girl I was talking to a minute ago, he said. She may be looking at me.

She may well be, Binder said, grateful to Vern for what must have been the first time in his life. However inadvertent it had been, Vern had taken the pressure off him, but the question was suddenly moot, for the girl turned and walked out into the night.

How about stepping out for a nip? Vern asked Binder.

Not right now, Binder said.

Vern was restless. The three of them seemed to confine him. He was soon up and drifting again, greeting people, shaking hands, like a host to a monstrous party. A rawboned young man in a denim suit asked Corrie to dance. When she smilingly declined he glanced halfquestioningly across the table and Ruthie arose a little unsteadily and took his arm and followed him to the dance floor.

What time is it? Binder asked.

Nearly ten, Corrie said, glancing at her wrist. Binder was instantly sorry he had asked. It had been a long summer. Corrie had patiently been ignored by him while he was writing, and Ruthie's promised visit and David's promise to take her to the Labor Day dance had helped her pass time through the sweltering summer. This was supposed to be more than a dance—it was a much-anticipated event. Now they both seemed to be turning sour for no reason.

Hey, you want to dance?

Not right this minute. We better sit here and keep an eye on Ruthie. She's getting high, I think.

When Ruthie returned, she and Corrie went off to find a ladies' room. Binder's head hurt worse. He watched Corrie's small dark form become swallowed in the crowd. He took four aspirin from a tin and swallowed them with Coke. When he glanced toward the door the flaxenhaired girl was there again, watching him with calm level eyes. He looked away. There was an eerie familiarity about her, as if she were a creation from his fantasies, from his dreams—or worse, he suddenly thought, fearing madness, from the book he was writing. The face was placid and smooth, seemed touched with the remnants of a lost, corrupt sweetness, a doomed innocence, and he knew irrevocably that he wanted her more than he had ever wanted anything. The book, Corrie, life itself.

She was gone before Corrie got back.

Ruthie wants you to go outside and look for Vern, Corrie told him. We didn't see him anywhere.

Likely he just went outside for a drink, Binder said. I didn't come here to babysit, he said to himself. Or did I?

He got up, moved through sweating shuffling couples into the night. The people were beginning to oppress him, to smother him, and outside the door he paused and breathed deeply, smelling the sere scent of Indian summer, becoming conscious of the wall of nightsounds beyond manmade noises, the crying whippoorwills and owls somewhere from a nightlocked hollow.

Vern wasn't in the car. There was a bottle in the front seat. Binder unscrewed the cap and drank, the brandy rushing down his throat like hot sweet fire. Binder looked about. Couples strolled armlinked in the dark, the night seemed alive with them. Beyond the glassed-in cars he could hear their murmuring voices, their faces floating together weightlessly like hungry creatures underwater or in a dream. He could hear a girl's protesting laughter from beyond the wall of pinewoods. As he turned back toward the building he heard a man's voice with an undercurrent of threat in it, felt simultaneously a hand on his arm. He stopped.

Hey, the blond girl said. She released his arm, reached a hand up to touch his beard.

Goddammit, Cissie, get over here, a man's voice said, and turning Binder saw between two parked cars a curious tableau: Vern leant backward across the hood of an orange Firebird, lying there unmoving and lax as if he had fallen asleep in this curious position. There were two men across from him, one draped against a truck door, arms crossed, the other facing Vern, standing almost between his feet. He was the redfaced man in the cowboy hat. He had an open knife in his hand. The girl drifted toward them.

Binder walked back to the car and unlocked the trunk. All he could find was a jack handle. He took it up and went back toward the Firebird, swinging the length of steel in his hands.

What's going on? Binder asked.

The man in the cowboy hat looked at him levelly. Nothing that concerns you very much, he said.

That's my brother-in-law.

What kin are you to that tire spud you got there?

Binder looked at it. There was an icy weight of panic at the pit of his stomach, and for a moment he'd forgotten the tire iron. He could feel the heavy dew cold through his sneakers.

Just close friends, he said.

Your friend here is all mouth and beltbuckle, the man said. I was just standin here wonderin what his insides was like.

What's your quarrel with him?

Why don't you ast him?

What the hell did you do, Vern?

Vern's voice sounded thick and peculiar. I never did a god-damned thing, he said. He raised a hand to wipe his mouth. There in the dark the smear of blood looked like ink.

He was foolin with my little sister was what he was doin. He had her out there in his big car feedin her whiskey.

I was talking to her was all I was doin.

Talkin, hell. He had his hand up her dress between her legs. I'm fixin to amputate that hand too, with no more deadenin than what he's already got in him.

Binder wondered vaguely about the law. Would there be any-body here? A constable, guard? Probably a bouncer was all, and with his luck this probably was the bouncer.

Look, Binder said. I don't know anything about this, but he didn't mean any harm. Let him up and he'll apologize to your sister and I'll get him in the car and away from here.

You want me to give him to you?

Yes.

All right, which piece do you want first? What are you anyway, his fucking lawyer?

Damn it, I'm trying to be as polite as I know how. I told you he's harmless.

Harmless, hell. Look at my little sister. She's simple. She ain't right in the head. She's like a kid, and him comin on to her like that, I'd a got there five minutes later he'd be needin a undertaker stead of a lawyer.

He's drinking, all he saw was a pretty girl.

I never meant any harm, Vern said.

The man stepped back. He closed the knife and lowered it. All right, he said. I want his sorry ass gone. You get him in that slick black car and haul him someplace out of my sight.

Vern straightened, slid off the car hood to the ground. His cowboy shirt had ridden up out of his jeans. He stood tucking it carefully into his belt. He looked as if he might say something.

Just go on and open your mouth one time, the man in the cowboy hat said. He looked at Binder. I ain't afraid of your goddamned tire spud, either.

Vern sidled away around the front of the car toward Binder. The man in the cowboy hat was watching them contemptuously. Jesus, he said. A hippie and the rhinestone cowboy. What'll wash up on Sinkin next?

At the car Binder opened the door and waited for Vern to get in. Vern stood stubbornly clinging to the door handle.

You want to get your ass in? I'll go get Corrie and Ruthie.

You told that son of a bitch I was harmless. The hell I am. I'm not harmless.

All right, Binder said tightly. I apologize. You're not harmless. You're a terror among men, and folks tremble at your footsteps. Now, you want to get in?

Vern got in and Binder closed the door. Stay there, he said as he walked back toward the music.

They rode in ghastly silence for a few miles. Ruthie's face was bright and accusatory. Then Vern seemed to regain his confidence. His mind began to rearrange events in a manner more to his liking, and he began to tell Ruthie and Corrie about it.

They doubled up on me, he said, two of them, both with knives. Hadn't been for David no telling what they'd of done. I'll tell you all a little secret. Deep down in my heart I always thought David was a smidgen chickenshit. But friends, he ain't. He'll hang right in there. Me and David make a good team, don't we, David. He whups the little ones and I get the big ones. Ain't that right, Binder.

Binder didn't say anything.

But what did you get into it about?

Hell, I don't know. They were drunk. I reckon they just wanted a fight and I was it.

Binder could feel Corrie's dark eyes on him, but he didn't look at her. He just watched the road ferrule in and out of deep hollows, drooping branches raking the car roof, the car rising over knolls shrouding ancient grownover graveyards, dark remote highrollers' houses. An orange harvest moon rode high over the dark ridges, flitted in and out of Binder's vision with the winding of the road.

When they were on the road to the homeplace, Corrie spoke for the first time. It's so lovely tonight, she said. This is the last of the summer. It's early, David. Can we stop by the creek a minute.

The silver moonlight was breathtaking. The night still held its warmth and the moon had ascended the tree line, spilling light indiscriminately over the landscape. The creek lay like a motionless river of quicksilver.

Vern was first out, clutching his bottle. By now the two were inseparable in Binder's mind. He could not imagine Vern with his mouth closed, or not clutching his bottle of peach brandy.

I got to see a man about a dog, Vern said thickly. He stumbled off toward a thick grove of sumac.

They got out and sat on the edge of the wooden bridge, peering down at the water. The surface was clear, motionless as a mirror.

Vern had come onto the bridge. He drained the bottle and dropped it into the creek, roiling the surface of the water. Binder wished he hadn't.

Yes sir, old David Binder knows how to go to one of these country dances, Vern said. With a jack handle in his hand, by God.

Corrie's face turned to Binder, her dark eyes wide, her face almost apprehensive, as if she were seeing suddenly a side of him she hadn't known existed.

You know what we ought to do? Vern asked them abruptly. We ought to go skinnydipping.

No, Corrie said quickly.

It's too cold, Ruthie said. I'm sleepy. Let's go to bed.

Chickens.

Binder was constantly amazed at how easily he could read Vern. His voice had been slurred and sly so that Binder wondered if he was as drunk as he acted, if he used it as an excuse for boorish behavior. He knew intuitively that this wasn't something that had suddenly occurred to Vern. He had been thinking of it for a time, perhaps two or three days. Perhaps since the day his gaze had lingered so lovingly on Corrie's crotch.

What a bunch of swingers, he said mockingly. Last one in's a rotten egg.

Binder got a cigarette out of the car and lit it. I never thought you would go to such lengths to see me naked, he said.

Always the smart mouth, Vern said.

In the stark clarity of the moonlight his face looked vacuous and haggard, less like a bored housewife's dream and more like a man drifting against his will aimlessly into middle age.

I don't know what it is about you that gets under my skin, Vern said. I've tried to be friends with you ever since we've been in the family. But forget it. I can't figure why you think you're such hot shit.

Vern, Ruthie said.

You shut up, Ruthie. You ain't got a damn thing. You ought to see my house in Orlando. It looks like a movie star's house. But you wouldn't be impressed. You'd be busy scribbling in your notebook. You wrote a book one time, and you think you're so damned smart. You been around so much. You act like me and Ruthie are hicks.

Binder drew on his cigarette, stared up the embankment toward the toolshed and beyond it the house. I didn't mean anything like that, he said. Absently he figured he might as well let Vern get it all said; he guessed it had been coming for a long time.

Orlando may not be New York City, but hellfire, we been around, me and Ruthie. We seen them X-rated movies. We been out with them swingers, too. Two or three times we been to parties where they swap up and—

Goddamn you, Vern, Ruthie said. Can't you just for once keep your mouth shut?

Hell yeah, we swapped and it was fun, too, and I was thinkin—

He stooped and leaned over Corrie, laid a hand on her shoulder, slid it to her bare arm. There was something possessive in his gesture, an attitude of dismissal toward Binder, as if he didn't count. She twisted her face up, her eyes enormous.

It was those eyes Binder saw when he hit him. He hit him hard in the stomach, taking care not to hit the beltbuckle. Vern folded forward, his stomach closing on Binder's fist. He slid to his knees and hunkered there, retching, trying to get his breath back.

Yeah, Ruthie said, circling Binder as if she were stalking him. Binder watched her warily. She looked as if she might scratch out his eyes. Yeah, beat up on a drunk man, will you? If Vern were sober—

Help me get him to the house, Corrie, Binder said. He hooked his hands beneath Vern's armpits and hoisted him to his feet. Vern stood swaying unsteadily, his curls all in his face.

Corrie was watching Binder apprehensively. She seemed near tears, didn't say anything. Past her dark head Binder could see the toolshed silhouetted against the sky. In the moonlight the worn old wood looked like hammered silver.

They lay in the darkness. Binder could hear the air conditioner whirring, feel Corrie's presence beside him in the bed. He wondered if she slept.

I shouldn't have hit him, Binder thought, only half-dreaming it. I ought to have let the hand play itself the rest of the way, at least looked at the rest of the cards. Maybe it wasn't just something Vern cooked up. Maybe I'm the point of conspiracy. Maybe the three of them had it planned. Maybe they want to draw old Binder out of his shell. I guess I missed my cue. Maybe I'm oldfashioned. Maybe I'm a stick-in-the-mud. Maybe I'm lost.

He turned to look at her face. It was vague and dreamlike, sleeping, the lashes dark and enigmatic on her cheeks. He thought of her eyes. The windows of the soul, the poet had said, but Binder knew there were always little cluttered attics. Dark, damp basements seething with vermin. Windowless little rooms the sunlight never hit.

Mornin, good buddy, Vern said.

Binder came out into the sun with his coffee cup in his hand. He sat on the stone doorstep. Vern, blinking against the day, came out the door behind him in a bright flowered shirt. He was contrite this morning, eager to please.

Last night seemed like a bad dream to Binder. It left a bad taste left in his mouth and his head still ached. He felt hungover and disoriented.

Ruthie and Corrie came out, moved lawnchairs into the sun.

What are you going to do this morning, David?

Binder set his coffee cup down. I'm going to walk back to the homeplace.

Mind if I walk back with you?

Binder did, but he said, No, it's fine with me.

Why don't we all go? Corrie asked. It's just this old houseplace that David says is haunted. He says positively awful things happened there. But I've been planning on digging up some more of those cannas. Is it okay if we do, David?

Binder shrugged. Why not?

I'll get a hoe, Vern said eagerly.

Binder put out his cigarette beneath his shoe. He turned. I'll get the hoe, he thought.

Vern was halfway through the wet grass to the toolshed. Binder followed him, quickening his pace.

He paused in the door for his eyes to adjust, but Vern was already in. He could hear him blundering around, kicking things out of his way. The halflight came into focus. Vern's flowered back leant to pick up the tamping bar, stooping toward the gaudy scrap of rag.

Vern, Binder said. Don't move.

Vern had seen it. He didn't move anything but his eyes, which sidled sickly sidewise, gleaming with panic, blind fear rising in them like water in a glass.

Don't even breathe, Vern.

The snake was coiled, her triangular head absolutely motionless, raised in the air a foot or so beside Vern's outstretched hand.

Vern was motionless as well, leant forward like a statue carved in an attitude of agony. Sweat beaded on his forehead. A crystalline drop crept out of the curls at his temple and down his cheek, hovered for a moment on his chin.

Do something, Vern whispered.

I wouldn't talk too much if I were you, Binder said. Snakes can't hear, but they can feel vibrations in the air. We can't have too many bad vibes here.

Kill it.

I aim to kill it, Vern. I'm just looking for something to kill it with.

He was looking for a piece of steel he could smash the snake's head with, or at least distract it until Vern could get out of the way. He paused for a moment, watching. Vern might have been leaning to stroke the snake. Or Corrie's arm, he thought suddenly, and saw quite clearly Vern's dark hand laid positively on Corrie's white arm, seeing not only that but Vern's face as well, Corrie's dark eyes turning up toward him.

What can I kill it with, Vern? Binder asked musingly. I can't find anything. Killing a snake. You need just the right tool...here's some onions, Vern. A world of onions. Do you reckon I could beat it to death with an onion?

What the hell's the matter with you, you son of a bitch?

I may have to go get a gun, Vern, Binder said. You just stay like you are. I been aiming to get a gun anyway.

He picked up a broken plowpoint, eased soundlessly toward the snake. As he was raising the steel, Vern's arm jerked involuntarily. He and the snake exploded into violent motion, Vern screaming and flapping his arm madly, the snake whipping back and forth, embedded in the flesh of his forearm, Binder trying to hit it as it flopped off. The snake struck the broken floorboard and

Binder hit it with the plowpoint, the creature coiling in on itself in agony, bright drops of blood spattered in the pillars of sunlight.

He stared in stricken disbelief as from the snake's mouth emerged a myriad of tiny, writhing baby snakes, perhaps a score of them, some already rusty miniatures of the mother, others almost glasslike, so translucent he could see the dusty floorboards through them. They fanned out on the planking, wriggling outward aimlessly in all directions from the epicenter of the dead snake's mouth.

Vern was on his hands and knees clutching his arm. You filthy son of a bitch, he said.

Binder went to the door.

Get the truck down here, he called.

Binder sat in the truck in the hospital parking lot. He seemed to have been waiting for a long time. The sun was hot through the glass. He lit a cigarette from the butt of another, leant to the mirror. He could see Corrie approaching, hear her heels hitting the asphalt. She got in.

How is he?

They're giving him antivenom. The doctors told Ruthie he'd probably be all right.

That's good, Binder said abstractedly. He was hot in the car, wanted to be in motion. Wanted to be back at the homeplace. He thought of the cool glade by the creek, the autumnal hills beyond it bright with maples like bursts of orange flames. The trees were turning already. Tomorrow there might be the year's first frost. He thought of the homeplace shrouded in snow, the road drifted deep, the place secure, inviolate.

Are they going back with us or what? Are we supposed to wait?

No, they're keeping him, David. He's too sick to go anywhere. And Ruthie…Ruthie's going to a motel. They're upset with you. Vern's awfully upset with you.

Vern's upset with me. Hellfire. I didn't bite him. The god-damned snake did.

He says you knew it was going to.

Going to. Fuck him. How do I know what a snake thinks?

She watched him in silence. Binder could feel the silence grow accusatory, could feel her rising concern for him. It did not move him, even touch him. He felt a cold remove from it, from her, from everything. It was all just yesterday's news.

From his childhood Binder had had the ability to look at himself with a cold and unflinching honesty, and he knew unquestioningly that he had changed. Winter ran in his veins and his insides were now chunks of bloody ice, and he knew he had crossed over into some foreign province of the heart, had left her more surely than he had ever feared her leaving him. He couldn't find his way back, but the worst part was knowing he would not come even if he could.

Queen of the
Haunted Dell

Queen of the Haunted Dell

An authenticated history of the night the Bell Witch followed us home

HERE'S WHAT HAPPENED OR MAYBE HAPPENED OR IS
SUPPOSED TO HAVE HAPPENED:

Adams, Tennessee, is in Robertson County, five miles from the
Kentucky line. In 1804, when John Bell moved his wife and six
children and slaves to a thousand-acre farm he'd bought on the
Red River, Adams was a virtual wilderness. Skirmishes with Indian
war parties up from the south were less than twenty years in the
past. The Indians didn't live here, but it was sacred ground to them
and had been for thousands of years, since the time of the Mound
Builders. It was also theirs by right of treaty. As was often the case,
the treaty had clauses and fine print and footnotes, and the land
was soon settled by prosperous white landholders, most of them
from North Carolina.

John Bell was prosperous, too, but he seems to have had a
clouded past. There were rumors of his being involved in the death
of his former overseer. By all accounts he was a close man in a
business deal as well, and it wasn't long before he found himself in
Robertson County civil court accused of usury in a slave trade with
a woman named Kate Batts.

These things about Bell, by the way, are not folklore or hearsay:
they're a matter of public record, but they are not mentioned in the

early books about the Bell Witch, which paint John Bell as a sort of stoic martyr.

Because of his legal trouble, Bell was excommunicated from the Baptist Church, and in a small community where almost every social function is tied in one way or another to the church, this was a big deal. Living in such a close-knit community of God-fearing folk, Bell must have felt like a pariah.

Then things got worse.

In 1817, John Bell saw an animal in his cornfield. It looked like a black dog but not exactly. When he fired his rifle, it vanished. Not long after, Betsy, Bell's thirteen-year-old daughter, was picking flowers and saw a girl dressed in green swinging by her arms from the branches of a tree. The girl in green vanished.

There were noises in the house. Something gnawing on the bedposts, rats maybe, the sound of something enormous and winged flying against the attic ceiling, the sound of chained dogs fighting. Lights flitted about the yard. Covers were yanked from folks trying to sleep. Hair was pulled, jaws slapped. Betsy seemed to catch the worst of it.

This went on almost every night for a year before Bell confided in anyone outside the family. According to M. V. Ingram's *An Authenticated History of the Bell Witch*, published in 1894 and based on an account written by one of Bell's sons, things had come to such a sorry pass—nerves were frayed, nobody was sleeping—that Bell had to have help and opinions. Two preachers were consulted, James Johnson and Sugg Fort.

Bell was a stern and autocratic man who had been able to keep the news of the disturbances confined within his family. But as soon as he confided in others, the cat, or whatever the hell manner of beast it was, was out of the bag and gone.

The self-styled investigators soon determined that there was an intelligence behind the phenomenon. It would respond to knocks and answer questions: one knock for yes, two knocks for no.

Odd as this may be, it did not set a precedent. A similar case had taken place in Maine in 1800. It happened again in Surrency, Georgia, and again in 1848 in Hydesville, New York, to a family named Fox. The Foxes were more amenable to this sort of thing, and within months they were holding séances and playing the ectoplasm circuit, giving birth to the great Spiritualist movement of the nineteenth century.

The witch—they had begun to call it this almost by default; no noun seemed adequate—thrived under all the attention she was getting. At night the yard would be full of wagons and buggies, the house full of folks putting the manifestations to the test. Apparently Bell turned no one away: he was hoping somebody could figure out all of this and put it to rest. So word spread, and the witch became a source of entertainment. Recreation was in short supply in Robertson County in 1817, and this was better than a pie supper, a church social, a cornhusking—as long as you could go home when the show was over and leave it where it was.

The Bell family couldn't do this. The witch seemed to have moved in to stay.

Then she developed a voice. First a sibilant whisper, then a strangled sort of gurgle. Eventually she began to sing gospel songs and to speak. From contemporary accounts (and there are a lot of them), the voice was very odd-sounding: metallic and somehow mechanical, it did not sound much like a human voice at all. From today's perspective it seems the witnesses were trying to describe a computer-generated voice, perhaps like the one in your telephone that asks you to punch a number for more information.

And information was what they wanted. *What are you? Where do you come from? What do you want?* they asked her.

There was no shortage of answers. In fact, she appeared a little perplexed herself. Pressed for the truth, she seemed not to know what she was, and as parapsychologists have discovered, if spirits exist, they're terrible liars.

I am a spirit that has always been and will always be, she told them. *I am everywhere and nowhere.* Or she was the spirit of an Indian whose bones they'd disturbed. Or she was the spirit of a man who had buried an enormous amount of money on the Bell farm and wanted them to find it. Finally she said: *I am no more or less than Kate Batts' witch, and I am here to torture and kill old John Bell.*

The Bell family came to refer to this four-year period as Our Family Trouble, and during that time there was a seemingly endless stream of folks arriving and departing. A few years before he became president, Andrew Jackson even considered it an adventure worthy of his reputation. He came with an entourage and wagons and tents and provisions, planning to stay a couple of weeks. But the spirit took offense to a professed "witch killer" they had brought along and ended up pulling his hair and humiliating him with slaps. After two days, the group unceremoniously packed up and left.

Many came intent on proving that the whole thing was a hoax. People had noticed that Betsy went into a trance before the entertainment commenced. The family thought of these as fainting spells, and it was only *after* Betsy came out of these trances that the spirit would speak. Some folks felt the spirit was drawing some sort of energy from her. Others decided that Betsy was a ventriloquist and that the whole thing was an elaborate put-on. But according to a contemporary account, a man once grasped Betsy and held a palm tightly across her mouth, and the voice went on unchanged and undeterred.

The entertainment apparently varied from the gospel to the X-rated and all points in between. The witch was a malicious gossip, and she delighted in relating the sexual doings of the crowd. Betsy was by now engaged to Joshua Gardner, and the spirit was fond of taunting Betsy with knowledge of indelicate matters that should have been private. The witch had a scatological sense of humor, and the house was often filled with the odors of vomit and excrement. If one can suspend disbelief long enough to picture it, the scene must have been like a rustic talk show, reality TV with an Early American motif and a disembodied host dealing in dirty linen and guilty secrets.

The witch had two stated purposes: to kill John Bell and to break up Betsy's impending marriage to Joshua Gardner. Bell died in 1820, a year before the cessation of the haunting. There is controversy about what he died from, but, predictably, the witch took credit, claiming that she had poisoned him. At his death, she filled the house with celebratory laughter and bawdy songs. According to Ingram's 1894 book, she sang "Row Me Up Some Brandy-o" at Bell's funeral.

Her energies seemed much dissipated by Bell's demise. Though a shadow of her formerly robust self, she still had the strength to prevent Betsy's marriage. To quote from the diary *Our Family Trouble* by John Bell's son Richard:

> Yet this vile, heinous, unknown devil, torturer of human flesh, that preyed upon the fears of people like a ravenous vulture, spared her not, but chose her as a shining mark for an exhibition of its wicked stratagem and devilish tortures. And never did it cease to practice upon her fears, insult her modesty, stick pins in her body, pinching and bruising her

flesh, slapping her cheeks, disheveling and tangling her hair, tormenting her in many ways until she surrendered that most cherished hope which animates every young heart.

The witch left in 1821, saying that she would return in seven years. According to John Bell Jr., she did reappear, but only to him, and only briefly. No one was interested in her anymore. She was yesterday's news, and the Bell family was weary beyond measure of the whole affair. Slighted, the voice promised (or threatened, perhaps) to return in 107 years.

By now the Bell children had largely dispersed into homes of their own on the original property. Betsy married her former schoolteacher and remained in Adams. Her mother, Lucy, stayed behind to live by herself in the old farmhouse. John Jr. lived in his own home across from her.

The rest is a matter of legal documents: marriages, probated wills, death certificates. After Betsy's husband died in 1848, she moved to Panola County, Mississippi. Lucy died in 1837, and the old log house was subsequently dismantled: no one would have it, and none of the Bells wanted to move back and live there.

But the story was too outrageous to die. In the 1850s, the *Saturday Evening Post* ran a story on the Bell Witch, postulating that Betsy was a ventriloquist and had faked the whole thing. Betsy sued for libel and won, settling for an undisclosed amount of money. Most of the family, as well as young Gardner, had scattered out of Adams County. It was as if everyone wanted some distance between himself and the growing legend.

In 1894, M. V. Ingram, after years of unsuccessful attempts, acquired the diary of Richard Bell and incorporated it into his *Authenticated History.* This account of the haunting was anathema to the remaining Bells as well as to their offspring, who considered the Family Trouble a shameful episode and their personal business. They were angry all over again in 1934 when Charles Bailey Bell published his own book, which included a recounting of his conversations with his great-aunt Betsy.

There are tales about bad luck following the Bells, about a family curse, but the history of any family is a history of death and misfortune.

So what, if anything but the birth of a folktale, happened?

Everyone who went looking for a solution found one, so there are ultimately more answers than questions and more culprits than victims.

1) It was a hoax perpetrated by Betsy Bell for reasons unknown, possibly a prank. She acquired the art of ventriloquism and put it to use.

2) It was a hoax perpetrated by one Richard Powell, who wanted to get rid of Joshua Gardner and John Bell and marry into the well-to-do Bell family.

3) It's true as told, and in the world as we know it there is no explanation.

4) Something happened, a poltergeist perhaps, but it's been grossly distorted by time and retelling.

5) It was black magic. Kate Batts *was* a witch, and this was her revenge on Bell.

6) Something happened. It's tied to a secret concerning Betsy Bell and her father, and the whole haunting is rooted in abnormal psychology.

7) The Bell farm is located on an ancient source of power, sacred to the Indians and whatever race came before them. Spirits have always been there, and they sometimes draw on energy wherever they can find it.

According to theories about poltergeists, an unhappy
household filled with adolescents would provide an
almost inexhaustible supply of energy. (It might be
worth pointing out that the spirit's powers waned as
Betsy passed from adolescence to womanhood.)

There are other explanations, but this seems sufficient.

The first possibility seems least likely if any weight can be
attached to newspaper accounts and sworn testimony. Hundreds of
people apparently witnessed her. They all can't be lying. As for the
second, it's hard to imagine how he did it, even if only a fraction
of the accounts are true. Also, motivation seems questionable, and
if you can sustain a practical joke for four years, naiveté must have
run deep in Robertson County.

The last two reasons are more interesting. Nandor Fodor was a
psychiatrist who investigated and wrote about poltergeists. In the
1930s and '40s he postulated that Betsy was sexually assaulted by
her father when she was a child. She repressed the memory, but
this repression erupted at the onset of puberty in violence against
her father. Fodor points out that the witch came down hardest on
Betsy and the elder Bell, implying at once that Betsy had feelings
of revenge and guilt: Bell had to die, and to punish herself Betsy
had to give up the man—Joshua Gardner—she loved.

But this theory isn't based on much, and Freudian psychology
isn't the gospel it once was. It's about as easy to believe in
malevolent spirits as it is disrupted psyches slamming things
around and poisoning folks. It also seems to me a little tacky to
accuse even a dead man of child molestation if you don't have the
goods to back it up.

Colin Wilson is a British philosopher and an investigator of
the paranormal. Poltergeists are pretty much his specialty, and he

started out believing the conventional theory about adolescent energy. But he came to think that teenage energy running amok didn't cover everything. He theorized that spirits that haunt places of power can utilize the frustrated energy of adolescents. Excess energy, violence, and unhappiness seem to provide a breeding ground for poltergeists and, Wilson says, spirits can come upon this energy and use it the way a child might kick around a football that he finds lying in a vacant lot.

In the end it seems you can twist the story to any frame of reference, hold it to the light, and turn it until it reflects whatever you want to see.

After the destruction of the Bell home, folks came to believe that the witch had taken up residence in a nearby cave, now called the Bell Witch Cave. The path to it is well traveled. It has been worn down by writers, reporters, television crews, parapsychologists, skeptics, true believers, and throngs of the merely curious. The path winds steeply down the face of an almost vertical bluff. The present owner of this section of the old Bell farm is Chris Kirby, and she's carrying a heavy-duty flashlight and leading the way. Underfoot is crushed stone, and the earth is terraced with landscape timbers to prevent the trail from eroding into the Red River, which is flowing far beneath us.

Past the guardrail you can see the river where the Bell sons used to flatboat produce down to the Cumberland and on to Mississippi and New Orleans. You can see the bench-like area of rock and brush that lies between the riverbank and the point where the bluff rises sheerly out of the bottomland. This is perhaps the only part of the Bell geography that remains virtually unchanged since 1817.

Betsy Bell, dubbed Queen of the Haunted Dell when she became the focus of the mystery, used to come here with Joshua

Gardner and other young people on lazy Sunday afternoons after the services at Red River Baptist Church. They'd fish in the river and picnic by the waterfall in the shade of the same huge oaks and beeches that are here now. At some point the young folks would separate into couples and go their own ways. Looking into the trees you can almost see them; your imagination can transform the sound of the waterfall into soft laughter.

At the mouth of the cave Chris turns toward us.

"People sometimes have problems photographing the entrance to the cave," she says. "Sometimes there's a mist that blocks the front of it, or maybe things that look like faces or orbs of light turn up in the pictures. Things that weren't there. Sometimes cameras just fail."

Thirty feet or so into the cave there's a heavy steel gate.

"People kept breaking in, and it's dangerous further back," Chris says, fitting a key into the padlock. "That's why you had to sign a waiver. Kids keep trying to slip in here with their girlfriends to scare them."

If fear is an aphrodisiac and if a tenth of the things told about the cave are true, then this is the ultimate horror movie.

Inside the cave the first thing you notice is the temperature. It's a constant fifty-six degrees, and the Bell family, among others, used to store perishables here. The second thing you notice is how impressively cave-like it is. This is no two-bit roadside attraction, no world's largest ball of twine, but a real cave, three stories laid one atop the other like a primitive high-rise, connected by crawl holes that wind upward through the first-floor ceiling.

"A kid got stuck in one back in the 1800s," Chris says, shining the light into a jagged ascending tunnel. "He was really stuck, he couldn't get out, and all at once a voice said, *Here, I'll get you out,* and the witch jerked him out. He was scared to tell his folks about it, but that night the witch told his mama, *You better put a harness on that boy so you can keep up with him.*"

Chris is fascinated by the Bell Witch story, and it's a fascination that predates her ownership of this cave. She's read all the books, and she says she's heard and seen a couple of things herself.

In the first large chamber there's a crypt perhaps a foot and a half wide by four and a half feet long, a child's crypt, chiseled out of rock. Large, flat rocks were shaped to fit vertically around the edges, and the body of a young Indian girl had been laid inside. More flat rocks for a lid, the hole covered over with a cairn of stone until a few years ago, when the cave's previous owner accidentally found it. The archaeologist who examined the bones said they were between two and three hundred years old.

If you can imagine someone laboriously chipping away at the rock and placing in the body, then it's not hard to see how private and personal this was, and suddenly it doesn't seem to be the sort of thing you should be paying five dollars to see.

In the next chamber Chris shows us where she saw a strange haze shifting in one corner. Farther back, five hundred feet or so into the bluff, the cave narrows until it's inaccessible. She shines the light. It's almost absorbed into the wet dark walls as the tunnel veers crookedly out of sight. You'd have to be a spelunker to crawl back in there.

"That's where I heard the scream coming from," Chris says. "Not any kind of animal, but a woman screaming. That's what that *Tennessean* camera crew heard, too."

We fall silent and listen, but all you can hear is the gurgling of underground water. If you listen intently enough, it becomes voices, a man and a woman in conversation, a cyclic rising and falling in which you can hear timbre and cadence but not the words, and in the end it's just moving water.

Outside in the hot sunlight you're jerked into another century.
Inside it was easy to feel that all these events were layered together
and happening simultaneously: the haunting, a wall smoked black
by Native American fires, the crypt of bones, the laughter of young
lovers exploring the cave. Outside it's just Adams, Tennessee, circa
2000, and a vague nostalgia for a place and time you've never been
and can never go.

Chris is locking up the cave. "Some people might talk to you,"
she says. "But a lot of people won't talk about it at all. After that
Blair Witch movie came out, this place was sort of overrun with
reporters and writers. But some people around here don't think it's
anything to joke about. Some of them have seen things and heard
things and feel the whole business should just be left alone."

"I don't really know what to think," Tim Henson tells me. "I know
something happened, but I've never really seen anything myself.
I've talked to a lot of people who say they have. A friend of mine
was fishing down in front of the cave and swears he saw a figure,
a human figure, that just disappeared. And people say they see
lights around that property. But I'm particular about finding an
explanation for things I see and hear. And so far I've always been
able to find an explanation that satisfies me."

Henson's the superintendent of the water department in Adams,
but he's also the town's unofficial historian, a walking encyclopedia
on the Bell family and their troubles, who can quote courthouse
records and church rolls from the nineteenth century without having
to look them up. He's the man that people come looking for when
they're doing a book or a documentary about the Bell Witch. Most
recently, he spent some time being interviewed for the Learning
Channel. Henson comes across as a shrewd and intelligent man, and
his take on the legend makes as much sense as any other I've heard.

"It doesn't matter to me if it's true or not," he says. "I guess *something* happened. There's about forty books now about it, and you don't write forty books about nothing. There's been three in the last year or so, and just the other day a fellow gave me a piece on the witch from an old 1968 *Playboy*. But I keep an open mind on all that. What I'm interested in is the story and the history, the Bells themselves and the way they interacted with their neighbors. There was a bunch of students down at Mississippi State University who tried to prove it was all a hoax, that Joshua Gardner hoaxed the whole county just to marry Betsy. But it's hard to say."

"But folks still believe in it here?" I asked.

"Oh yes. Some do. And they figure it's not too smart to make fun of it or to get into it too deep. There was a couple here, a descendant of John Bell and one from Joshua Gardner. They fell in love and courted all their lives, but they were afraid to marry because of the Bell Witch."

When I was kid I read an issue of *Life* magazine about the seven greatest American ghost stories, and that was the first time I heard of the Bell Witch. Later my uncle, who was a great storyteller and had read the early books, fleshed out the tale. I found the books and read them myself, and for my money it's the quintessential ghost story. I figured that someday I'd go to Robertson County and see the Bell farm, which seemed to me an almost mythic place existing only in its own strange fairytale geography.

It was years before I made my first visit, more years still before I made my second.

The first I made with my uncle, whom I held in great esteem. I was beginning to read Steinbeck and Algren, and he seemed to be one of their characters come to life. He was sort of a restless-footed hard drinker, hard traveler, barroom brawler. Plus he had a tattoo on his bicep: a dagger with a drop of blood at its tip, a scroll wound round the blade that read DEATH BEFORE DISHONOR. He had lied about his age to get into World War II, then crouched seasick and heartsick in the prow of a landing craft while the beaches at Normandy swam toward him like something out of a bad dream. He fought yard by yard across France and was wounded at the Battle of the Bulge. He was a hero, and he had the medals to prove it, though he didn't think they amounted to much.

After the war he bummed around the country, working where he could and riding freight trains, sleeping sometimes in places you don't normally want to associate with sleeping: jails, boxcars, graveyards. He was an honest and an honorable man, but he'd been down the road and back. He was what they used to call "a man with the bark on."

By the time we rode out to the Bell farm, a lot of time had passed, and he had settled down, quit drinking, and become a respectable family man.

At the time the cave was private property (it still is, but it's set up as a tourist attraction), and we weren't allowed to see it, let alone go inside. So we talked to a few locals, went looking for the graveyard and whatever remnants of Bell's old log home might remain. The graveyard is in a cedar grove a mile or so off US 41, and it's not easy to find. But it's been found time and again by vandals, who stole Bell's original tombstone and even dug up some of the graves. All that remains of the house are a few of the stones it used to stand on.

It was dark before we found our way out of the woods, and though we were trying to maintain a degree of detached curiosity, it was undeniable that this was an eerie place.

A few months later my uncle and his wife turned up at my house in the middle of the night with a strange tale. He looked nervous and haggard, far from the cool and collected man I was accustomed to. Something had jarred him, and he didn't take long getting around to it.

"That thing has followed me home," he said.

Life had gone on, and I didn't know what he was talking about. "What thing?"

"That Bell Witch, or whatever it is. We keep hearing things, seeing things. It's about to drive us crazy."

"What kind of things?" I asked.

"We've heard voices. People mumbling, but you can't hear what they're saying. A hell of a racket that sounded like you'd dropped a chest of drawers from the ceiling and smashed it on the floor. You go look and there's nothing there. The other night I looked out the kitchen window and saw this ball of blue light just rise up from the ground and move off into the woods."

I didn't know what to say.

"We want you to sleep in that bedroom where we hear that stuff," he said. "If you hear something, at least we'll know we're not going crazy."

There was no way I wanted to do that. But by now I was trying to get down the road and back myself, and I had a reputation to maintain. I was also hoping this would turn out to be his idea of a practical joke.

"All right," I said.

This is what I heard, or think I heard:

I couldn't sleep, and I kept a light on. At about three in the morning I was reading an old copy of *Reader's Digest* when I heard a chuckle, a soft, malicious chuckle of just a few seconds' duration. It seemed to come from no particular point in the room.

I thought it was a joke. I jerked open the bedroom door. There was no one there. I went through the house. Everyone was asleep.

It was a long time until daylight.

What did I hear? I don't know. Did I really hear it at all? I don't know that, either, and I wouldn't argue it either way. It doesn't seem to matter. You hear what you believe you hear.

My uncle lives in West Tennessee near a town named after Joshua Gardner's brother, and I called him the other night.

"Did you really hear all that stuff in that house, or were you just pulling my leg?" I asked him.

"We heard things right up until we sold the place and moved," he said. "It sort of died down, but every now and then we'd hear something. You'll notice nobody lives too long in that house. It's changed hands several times since we sold it."

I told him I had been back to Robertson County and that I was writing an article about the Bell Witch.

"It might be best to leave that stuff alone," he said.

I don't know if there's any truth in all this business. Because almost two hundred years have passed since the original haunting supposedly occurred, I don't suppose anyone else will know. But I do know that the world is a strange and wondrous place. There are mysteries on every side if you care to look. I also know that I don't know nearly as much now as I thought I did at twenty-five. If I stacked the things I know next to the ones I don't, I wouldn't have a very tall stack.

Every question is multiple choice, and truth depends on your frame of reference. It sometimes seems an act of hubris to even form a conjecture.

I'd leave that stuff alone, I heard time after time from one source or another, and it might be worth remembering that the Bell Witch saved her strongest malice for scoffers and debunkers. It might be wise to keep one's disbelief to oneself.

On the other hand, she was clairvoyant. So it might be best not to think about that stuff at all.

A Note from the Publisher

Steven Gillis, publisher of Dzanc Books, wishes to acknowledge the many people who have helped make this book possible. *Little Sister Death* was found among William Gay's literary archive after his death. A team of William's friends, including J. M. White, Shelia Kennedy, Susan McDonald, Lamont Ingalls, and Paul Nitsche, compiled and transcribed William's remaining works from his handwritten notebooks and a typescript found among his papers. *Little Sister Death*, the first of several planned posthumous releases, was then passed to Guy Intoci and Michelle Dotter at Dzanc Books. The original papers can be found at the Sewanee University Library Special Collections.